William A. Jansen

Modern Medical Miscellany

Health for the millions - a collection of practical hints and instructive facts regarding

our physical welfare and spiritual happiness

William A. Jansen

Modern Medical Miscellany
Health for the millions - a collection of practical hints and instructive facts regarding our physical welfare and spiritual happiness

ISBN/EAN: 9783337390617

Printed in Europe, USA, Canada, Australia, Japan

Cover: Foto ©Andreas Hilbeck / pixelio.de

More available books at **www.hansebooks.com**

Modern Medical Miscellany;

OR,

HEALTH FOR THE MILLIONS.

———

A COLLECTION OF

Practical Hints and Instructive Facts Regarding Our
Physical Welfare and Spiritual Happiness;

WITH A SUPPLEMENT ON

HYGIENE IN MATRIMONY,
CHOICE OF SEX, EASY CONFINEMENTS, ETC.,
ON RATIONAL PRINCIPLES.

—— ———

BY

WM. A. JANSEN

Formerly Physician to the Orange Mountain Sanitarium,
Associate Physician to the Glen Haven Hydro-Thera-
peutic Institute, and to the Northampton
Retreat for Chronic Invalids.

———

MIAMISBURG, OHIO:
THE HEALTH-REFORM PUBLISHING CO.
1892.

TO

James Caleb Jackson, M. D.,

One of the stanchest pioneers for truth reform and
hydrotherapy, now Nestor of that school,
His Generous Friend and Preceptor,

This work is
appropriately and respectfully
Dedicated by

The Author.

In working out the problem of a *multum in parvo* on Health, Hygiene, and Physical Culture, we derived considerable assistance from the writings of our friends and former colleagues Drs. Chas. W. Grau, Robert Wesselhoeft, and R. T. Trall, including translations of I. H. Rausse. We also received valuable aid of D. H. Jacques on "Physical Perfection," and some biographical data were drawn from the publications of Dr. M. Roth and Major Rothstein. Brief quotations of others have been credited where used.

W. A. J.

PREFACE.

" By no other means can man approach nearer
to the gods, than by conferring health on man."
—*Cicero.*

IN view of the great flood of books on health, on sanitary
reform, or public and domestic hygiene, during these literary storms it should be requisite of every new publication,
occupying the same field, to present proof of its right to
be, its claim and privilege to live and prosper. This little
volume, we believe, possesses the vitality to comply with
these conditions. It appeals to a large circle of readers, and
will offer wholesome advice and valuable instruction to
them all. Speaking in plain and popular terms, it will
avoid all high technical entanglements. Its author has
forty years of medical training, and has passed through an
extensive field of observation. This work will be found
brimful of new ideas, while some ideas not entirely new
have been interwoven for the simple reason that certain
doctrines may be repeated again and often, as they seem to
be important, and their great truths, as those of the Scrip-
tures, are an everlasting force and moral influence.

Why is it, we ask, that in this, our age of progress, intellectual growth in all departments of science, and general
enlightenment, so many people suffer from sickness, chronic
disorders of the system, nervousness, or periodical ennui?
Among the most mischievous influences of the time is the
morbid haste to accumulate. Health is recklessly sacrificed
in the acquisition of wealth, or of public honors, or political

power—as the means to the same end mostly. Yet, there is this difference between these two temporal blessings—health and money: Money is the most envied, but really the least enjoyed; health is the most enjoyed, but the least envied, and the superior value of the latter is still more obvious when we discover that the poorest man would not part with good health for money, while the richest often would part with all their surplus cash for robust health.

Another great enemy to health is our present system of education, the hot-house pressure and haste now in vogue in nearly all the institutions of learning, especially those for girls, without any regard to their physical well-being whatsoever. The future mothers of this nation are daily slaughtered for imaginary glory, or, what is worse, to serve as temporary advertisements for our "female colleges."

To regain health, if lost or impaired, to fortify its possession if it is ours, will be the aim of these pages. The directions and advice offered are in accordance with modern progress in treating diseases; they exclude drug-medication, and forcibly appeal to the common-sense movement of the nineteenth century, presenting therapeutics (curative means or remedies) in two grand divisions—water and exercise, or hydro-therapeutics and gymnastics, in all their branches, including scientific or medical gymnastics, the Swedish movements as invented by Ling, etc. It is hardly possible for anyone to peruse the lines of this work without being paid for time and money invested a hundredfold. This little Health Gospel should be in the hands of every intelligent reader.   W. A. J.

MIAMISBURG, OHIO, 1892.

CONTENTS

PAGE

Gymnastics—Their Origin and Importance. The
Muscular System—Its Regulated Activity a
Condition of Robust Health........................ 9–28
Hydro-Therapeutics and Their Relation to Gym-
nastics, or, Vinzenz Prisznitz and Peter Henry
Ling 29–38
Massage—Its Proper Definition, Its History and
Application... 39–43
The Russian Government and Its Great Interest
in Medical Reform.................................. 43–45
Prisznitz as a Man and a Physician, and Captain
R. L. Claridge, of the English Army........... 45–51
Sir Bulwer Lytton and His Personal Experience
under Hydro-Therapeutics........................ 52–70
Baron Von Liebig's Researches on the Chemistry
of Food.. 71–73
Dr. Pereira on Opium and Mercury.......... 78–79
Dr. Radcliffe, about Physics and Physicians...... 80
Faith-Cure and Faith-Doctors 81–86
"The Physician Himself"............................ 86–91
Natural Length of Human Life.................... 91–95
The Exercise and Practice of Swimming as a Phy-
sical Accomplishment, as a Therapeutical
Agency, and an Orthopedic Gymnastic......... 95–99
The Natatoria of the Government at West Point
and Annapolis... 99–101
Horseback-Riding and Its Great Sanitary Im-
portance... 101–108

vii

PAGE.

Rowing, Bicycling, Skating, Lawn-Tennis, Croquet, etc., Considered as Gymnastics...................... 109

Hygiene—Public and Domestic. The Air We Breathe...................... 110–114

Observation In the Field—Hospitals During Our Civil War...................... 114–116

The Clothes We Wear, with Special Reference to Underwear...................... 116–122

The Food We Eat...................... 122–126

Frederick the Great, and Alexander Von Humboldt...................... 126–127

American Pork and Lard at Berlin and Vienna... 129

Dr. Beaumont, of United States Army, and His Investigations on the Person of Alexis St. Martin...................... 132–134

Food-Resources—Present and Future............... 134–136

Drinks, Natural and Artificial...................... 136–142

Adulteration of Water...................... 143–144

Purification of Common Water...................... 144

Milk as a Drink, and as an Article of Diet........ 144–149

Of Light and Its Influence on Health............... 149–151

Air Baths and Sun Baths...................... 151–153

Of Sleep and Its Necessity...................... 153

Tobacco as a Poison...................... 157–160

Will in Disease...................... 160–173

The Last Period of General Grant's Life as an Honorable and Valuable Illustration............ 174–175

Hygiene in Matrimony. Its Enforcement Our Future Salvation...................... 175–181

Stirpiculture as Applied to the Human Family.. 181–190

Gestation and Confinements Made Safe and Easy.. 190–193

Midwives—Male and Female...................... 193

Choice of Sex...................... 204–210

Appendix...................... 211

MODERN MEDICAL MISCELLANY.

PART I.

Gymnastics—Their Origin and Importance—The Muscular
System—Its Regulated Activity a Condition of Health.

ONE of the most impressive features of our
present hyper-civilization is the constant contra-
diction between the better knowledge of mankind
and the actions committed in direct opposition
to their moral convictions. Everybody admits
that there is the most admirable connection, as
well as a wonderful action and reaction, between
soul and body; so much so, that never one sickens
without involving immediately the other. "*Mens
sana in corpore sano*"[1] expresses the same idea,
only reversing the premises, and is a truth acknowledged from antiquity up to modern days.
Furthermore, it is equally admitted that powers
of whatever kind, bodily or mental, only exist
when constantly exercised, and that inactivity
likewise destroys the action of the body, as of

---

[1] "A sound mind in a sound body," or "No soundness of mind
without soundness of body."

the soul. Nay! inactivity and inertness of the body alone excludes action of the mind, and makes it gradually relapse into the torpid slumbers of imbecility.

Notwithstanding that both these truths are universally admitted, they are most frequently neglected and sinned against. Many persons concentrate all their action and energy upon mental pursuits, and are sorely punished for overlooking the claims of the bodily half. The reverse is not met so frequently, on account of the naturally greater activity and versatility of the mind, except in a somewhat modified form; that is, the prevailing desire to enjoy sensual pleasures, the overtaxing of the capacity and endurance of the digestive and other organs, and in consequence, likewise, the sad ruin and havoc in the body first, and, secondarily, of the mind soon after.

The omission of the development of the body, and of those vital processes which only exist by the simultaneous exercise of all faculties, viz., the change and formation of matter in our system, proves the cause of many diseases and deaths everywhere. The physicians of all ages and countries recommend adequate bodily exercises, in particular to those of their patients who follow professions, or a mode of life that excludes the sufficient use of the bodily faculties. Walking, traveling on foot, riding on horseback, garden work, and many other labors, down to wood-sawing, have been resorted to, but all these modes of exercise, although excellent and most wholesome in themselves, are either too uniform in their effect or consume too much time, in order to produce the desired result, and are generally soon discontinued. Even walking, which most frequently among them is kept up, seems hardly sufficient and rather too limited in its extent over the various portions of the muscular system. Four to eight hours of brisk walking, or the same time spent in outdoor labors is by no means excessive, but can be carried out easily and for any length of time; yet the total amount of muscular exercise involved is not too much, but might be considered sufficient to sustain full vigor of health. But how few are able to carry this into effect, chiefly when our present state of civilization requires more time for the development and application of mental labor with the majority of individuals. Besides, who would feel inclined, for any period of time, to consume daily a number of hours in walking, etc., without a more direct purpose, and in all sorts of weather?

To meet these difficulties many means have been invented, in order to concentrate the intensity of exercises, and to perform more in quantity during a limited space of time. In this way gymnastics originated, and by this means the necessary amount of muscular exercises can be realized in a quarter or half an hour, allowing business men, and others who can or will not employ more time for out-door exercise, to have sufficient and varied muscular activity.

We might consider these gymnastics, as far as they are connected with the art of the physician, medical gymnastics, presenting a double point of view. First, therapeutic exercises, as far as they are calculated to remove existing diseases and anomalies, with the special sub-division of orthopedic exercises, when directed against the various deformities of the human body, innate or . acquired. Secondly, hygienic exercises, as far as they are calculated to prevent diseases, to preserve health and vigor up to old age, and to insure a sound and normal development of the growing body. Therapeutic gymnastics were naturally at first employed against such chronic and feverless diseases, the original cause of which was found in deficient bodily activity, but soon thereafter it was discovered that their use could be successfully extended over a large number of other derangements, originating from various causes. That this has been at times carried too far, as in case of **Dr.** Winship and his system of concentrated lifting exercises, and by other fanatics who extol certain gymnastics as a universal panacea, does not speak against them, but against those advocates, by overrating a most energetic and valuable remedy, which, properly employed, has been of immense benefit to suffering mankind, and in many cases of dreadful disease has proven itself the only way to health. A universal medicine or method of resisting or curing all diseases, the many advertisements and assertions of charlatans, quacks, and nostrum-mongers to the contrary notwithstanding, is impossible, on account of the complicated structure of our organization, and consequently of the manifold variety of its diseases, the features of which might be different and require special attention in every individual!

Gymnastics, properly circumscribed and intelligently applied, prove in many instances a true and valuable agency, a real acquisition, which, under frequent circumstances, cannot be replaced by any other means whatever known. In order to understand the curative effects of therapeutic gymnastics in general, it is necessary that we first explain to ourselves the physiological importance of the motive organs—the muscles, and acknowledge their vital part in the total economy of our organization.

The structure of our body being calculated for a free and full activity in all its parts, they cannot gain their proper development or enjoy their normal state of health without an amount of bodily and mental action corresponding with their individual powers.

Motion and action of the voluntary muscles—in other words, full bodily activity, is even the most necessary of the two, as we will show by the manifold favorable effects it produces.

The fundamental condition of all organic life is the uninterrupted renovation of substance, comprising the generation of new material out of the nutriments and inhaled air, and the excretion of old matter worn out and decomposed by the vital process. The more this process of mutual exchange of matter is animated, within certain natural limits, the more life itself gains in vigor, freshness, and duration, while all hindrances or interruptions in this act of constant renovation and rejuvenation cause indisposition, destruction, death, unless they are soon equalized again. Insufficient consumption of substance, or again insufficient excretion of worn-out and useless particles, their retention in the system, as well as an impaired balance in the reception and want of aliments, is the most common cause of irregularities in the development and course of human life. This constant change of matter is based upon the full activity of all the organs of the body, alternating in proper ratio with intervals of rest.

The muscles are not only the most extensive of all systems of the body, their aggregate weight amounting to more than one-half, but they are also the most lively ones, therefore consuming matter in a higher degree and faster than any other, as it is their office to move the whole bulk of the body by contraction of their fibers; and this voluntary locomotion is undoubtedly the principal faculty of animal life. For both these reasons, being the most voluminous, and consuming its substance most rapidly, the muscular system is preëminently fitted to enhance, by its full or increased activity, the general change of matter in the most rapid, powerful, and perfect manner, and by this the totality of vital processes is invigorated and animated, the regeneration and purification of the blood and other liquids likewise insured. As the blood is the universal source of nutrition for all parts of the organism, and, because the action of the muscles reflects itself in an increased afflux of blood to themselves, the whole circulation, generation, and mixture of this fluid of life is improved, whence again follows an increase of digestion, respiration. all the secretions and excretions,—in short, of the totality of organic life.

The free use of our muscles immediately enlivens and increases the number and strength of the pulsation of the heart, the development of animal heat, the desire for food and drink, the secretions of the skin and kidneys, and insures a sound and refreshing sleep.

Daily observation shows that the muscular substance itself grows more full, firm, and hard through systematic exercise, while the deposits of useless fat and cellular tissue disappear: a substance of higher order is, therefore, developed at the expense of lower ones. In this way the muscular action proves to be the agent to remove old decaying particles out of the blood and to replace them with new ones, full of vitality. Thus it becomes evident that the accumulation of those morbid particles in the system which deposit themselves upon different organs as causes for disease, can be prevented by exercises intelligently applied, or even removed if already accomplished; consequently, the disease already seated will be cured. Another point might be added, of more importance than does appear to the superficial observer : the general increase of circulation toward the periphery, the gentle friction of body and clothes during exercise, increases the perspiration, thus strengthening the capillary action, assisting the skin to throw off its morbid obstructions. It is generally not understood that the skin is an organ, very important in its functions; not a mere cover or shelter for the body within. This fact, though, is easily comprehended when we consider that through its action in normal or healthful condition it carries off three-fifths of all the waste of the body. A more complete examination of this subject will be found in another part of this work.

Of course we must not overlook that such curative efforts also require that other conditions of life besides should be well regulated, and that in addition, nature may frequently require varied assistance for a perfect restoration of health. Certainly muscular activity, well calculated and well adapted to the individuality of the case, exists as one of the principal and most natural, and at the same time most powerful, therapeutic agencies.

Of the diseases to which this system and its treatment are chiefly adapted, and for which it has been acknowledged and proven itself eminently successful, we will mention: All chronic abdominal diseases, with their various forms of consequences,—that frequent curse of the present human race. Abdominal plethora, torpor and

2

stagnation of liver and spleen, hemorrhoids, etc., are removed by an increased and reëstablished circulation. Congestion to the head, hypochondria, and melancholy disappear, the different processes of digestion are animated, dyspepsia and habitual constipation, as well as chronic diarrhœa, are promptly cured. The contractile fibers of the abdominal muscles are strengthened, and by a reflective action upon the involuntary muscular fibers of the stomach and intestines, the latter will recover their tone and vitality, the body, in particular hands and feet, cease to show coldness, that permanent symptom of dyspeptic agony. Another way by which muscular exercise produces curative effects, is the intimate relation between the muscular and nervous systems; or, in other words, the influence of the motory nerves upon the sensitive ones and their centers. The former, being a part of the muscles, might be considered identical with them.

The feeling of perfect ease and bodily comfort is based upon a normal and healthful state of the nervous system, and in particular, upon a perfect balance in the state of excitation and action between all its single parts. If the motory system rises above its equilibrium, it is done at the expense of the sensitive one, and it can only be reduced again by the opponent being equally raised. On this relation are based the invigoration, the calming in a state of over-excitement, the exhilaration of mind, produced by appropriate exercises.

By dynamic influences, muscular action produces the equilibrium between the nerves of motion, sensation, and nutrition,—the latter also called the sympathetic ones,—while continued inactivity of the muscles causes an accumulation of the nervous power, or congestive conditions of the nervous fluid in the central organs, brain, spine, and ganglia. These congestions increase the normal sensation to a morbid sensibility, and derange the whole process of nutrition and assimilation in the abdominal sphere.

We gain also a great remedy and valuable adjuvant in the treatment of weakness and dullness of the nervous system in all its branches, such as muscular paralysis and its various consequences; spinal curvatures, chicken-breast, atrophy of single limbs or separate groups of muscles; also, irritability and perversed sensibility of the nerves, in the shape of hypochondria and hysteria, spermatorrhea, certain mental irritations, chronic spasmodic diseases, as St. Vitus's dance, epilepsy, neuralgia, and rheumatism.

We cannot omit here to mention the important fact, that the mind itself gains considerably by regular exercise of the will, while producing definite bodily actions, while struggling against and conquering relaxation, stiffness, or laziness of the body. The volition in general is strengthened; energy, perseverance, hope, and mental courage are imparted, and moral sluggishness removed, which so often annihilates the effect of the best and most rational treatment in chronic diseases. In reality, there is no greater enemy to all honest physicians and their endeavors, than the want of courage and strength of will[1] to recover, on the part of the patient; wherein, at the same time, lies the reason why so few physicians like to occupy themselves with the treatment of chronic derangements of the nervous system.

The influence of muscular action increases the strength and elasticity even of the bones and articular ligaments, and the mechanical effect on the forces of certain parts of the body is very important, and cannot be supplied by any other means whatever, least of all by *so-called supporters*, and other kind of machinery and bandages. That the latter even *increase the difficulty* by suspending the natural action of muscles more or less, can readily be proven. The structure of the human skeleton and the arrangement of the

[1] A separate chapter on will-power and its weighty importance in sickness will be presented in another part of this work.

muscles supporting it, are of such a nature that the development and contractibility of these various groups of muscles materially aid its position and arched structure, especially in the upper part of the trunk, the chest.

A great number of diseases are caused, materially, by an impaired or irregular space being allowed to the organs in the chest and abdomen, which are all of the most vital importance for life and health. This is easily understood if we observe that in many persons the large muscles of the arm, which are attached all around the chest, connecting with the intercostals, and greatly influence its shape and capacity, are hardly ever called into full and perfect activity.

Now, if we intend to procure to those organs, mechanically narrowed in, displaced, and hindered as they are, their natural freedom and action; or, if this should be impossible, to its full extent, if we at least wish to ease and comfort them in their arduous duties, the enlargement and improvement of those cavities is the first and most important condition To procure it, proper gymnastic treatment alone furnishes the means. We there through muscular action produce mechanical extension and compression, partly on single portions, partly on the whole chest, enlarging its cavity, equalizing both its sides, and correct all the abnormal dimensions of the whole structure and insure the permanency of these improvements. Those who may yet doubt these possibilities, we can assure that we observed frequently and in hundreds of cases, where in a few months, even after deducting the increase of muscular tissue, the circumference of the chest had been increased several inches. How much the cubic space for the lungs must have gained, can be readily calculated. As diseases which derive prompt benefit from this particular change, we may enumerate: Insipient tubercular consumption, emphysema of the lungs, several forms of asthma, and heart troubles, derangements of the stomach, liver, displacements in females, and many external deformities.

If we consider the life, chiefly of the higher classes of society, we find that a large majority of persons, without being really sick, suffer from want of exercise, by either not using the right mode or a sufficient quantity of it. Where walking alone is resorted to, three large groups of muscles are entirely neglected in their development, and consequently exist only in a crippled state, although they are of the utmost importance in the economy of the bodily household, and each of them stands in close rapport with a number of other functions of the greatest necessity to health

and life. We will name first, the muscles of the
chest, on account of inactivity of the arms. These
muscles not only move the upper extremities, but
serve for the rhythmic enlargement and contraction of the chest, by which the respiration is
produced, chiefly, the most important part of it,
the inspiration. Upon our breathing depends
the circulation of the blood through the lungs, and
consequently, the exchange between blood and
atmosphere, by which the former is renewed and
enlivened. The importance of these functions is
easily shown, as we perish if it is interrupted only
for a few minutes. With the perfection and
extent of the respiration correspond the energy
and vivacity of the whole life, but want of
systematic exercise in general, of the armmuscles
in particular, weakens the breathing and makes it
much less extensive.

Not only must we procure pure and wholesome
air to our lungs, but it must also be introduced in
sufficient quantity, and the latter is only possible
if all respiratory muscles are in full activity and
vigor. It may be proper here to show how the
extent and perfection of breathing can be judged
by the proportionate numbers of strokes of the
arterial pulse and respirations in a given time. In
persons with normal and vigorous lungs, six and
seven pulsations coincide with one respiration,

while in feeble persons with impaired breathing, this proportion often sinks as low as three to one.

Secondly, the abdominal muscles with their tendons. They assist and animate, by their voluntary contractions and natural elasticity, the functions of the organs, enclosed in that cavity, as digestion, circulation, excretions, parturition, etc. At the same time they protect these organs and secure them in their proper places, during violent movements and concussions. Finally, they co-operate in the expiration and similar movements, as speaking, laughing, coughing, etc. Their neglected development or laxity produces many derangements, as torpidity and interruption of all the above named abdominal functions, ruptures, and other displacements of vital organs. One of the chief reasons for the injurious results of sedentary habits is, that in sitting the abdominal muscles relax and cease to exercise that certain pressure on the organs enclosed in this cavity, which seems to be very essential for their functions.

Third and finally, the spinal muscles suffer for want of action and movement of the trunk. It is their office to strengthen and support the spine, bend it sideways, assist in various other motions, as well as in inspiration and expiration. Their action is important, as their weakness not only injures the shape of the back and body, but also, as the bending of the former diminishes the size of the caverns for lungs and abdomen, produces all the troubles and consequences from compression mentioned above. Most of the curvatures of the spine result from debility or inactivity of these muscles.

The spine forms the central line and universal support for all the movements of the body and its members; so much so that these movements cannot be properly executed unless the spine is straight, firm, and healthful. We are far from asserting the want of exercise to be the sole cause of all these dreadful enemies of happiness and life itself, but certainly do not assert too much if we ascribe to it a great share in their creation. Even persons who are not visited quite so severely through the neglect of bodily training and systematic exercise, grow old and dull before their time and suffer from many deformities and debilities. Especially, the female sex would not decay so early, but preserve the bloom of youth, if it could be induced to take more active exercise. We might dwell on this subject more extensively, but hope we have succeeded by the foregoing sketch to convince the reader of the full importance of hygienic and therapeutic gymnastics as here defined.

Plato says: "The excess of bodily exercises

may render some of us wild and unmanageable, but the excess of arts, sciences, and music makes us too faddled and effeminate; only the right combination of both makes the soul circumspect and manly."

Galen, the celebrated physician, says "that if diseases take hold of particular parts of the body, and fix themselves there for any length of time, there is nothing more efficacious or more sure to drive out the enemy from his position than diligent exercise and systematic use of our limbs."

Herodicus, the great teacher of Hippocrates, cured himself (and others) of a continued predisposition to disease by gymnastics, and, notwithstanding his many interruptions of good health, reached the age of a hundred years.

Hoffman, who cites Avicenna, Sanctorius, and Lord Bacon, declares "gymnastics to be almost a universal medicine, because there is no disease, he says, whose farther development could not be checked, or which could not, at its commencement, have been cured by a well-informed and judicious course of bodily exercise."

Montaigne, the able philosopher, says: "It is the soul, not a body only, which we have to educate; it is a man of whom we must not make two, not train the one without the other, but must guide and lead them like a pair of horses harnessed to one shaft."

Rousseau says: "All sensual passions are found in effeminate' bodies; the more they are roused, the less they can be satisfied. A weak body weakens the mind." And again: "If you wish to develop the mind, develop the power which that mind has to govern. Exercise your pupil's body, make him healthy and strong, that you may make him prudent and reasonable."

"Die Thätigkeiten des Körpers entsprechen den Thätigkeiten des Geistes; jede Ueberspannung von Geistesthätigkeit hat eine Ueberspannung körperlicher Actionen zur Folge, so wie das Gleichgewicht des ersteren oder die harmonische Thätigkeit der Geisteskräfte mit der vollkommensten Uebereinstimmung des letzteren vergesellschaftet ist. Geistige Lust hat jederzeit eine thierische Lust, geistige Unlust eine thierische Unlust zur Begleiterin."—*Schiller.*

But while we cannot shut our eyes to the immense advantage resulting from gymnastic training, we must not, on the other hand, be seduced and blinded by enthusiasm for the good cause so far as to believe that the advantage is in proportion to the increased quantity. Only the right measure—the proper amount of physical force expended—is the wholesome one; these exercises must be regarded only as the means for the attainment of higher aims, and not the aim itself. This refers emphatically to pedagogic gymnastics as practiced at the present time at some of our colleges and universities. The bodily training at these institutions is excessive and oftentimes too one-sided. Their rivalry in rowing, football, and otherwise healthful sports is overdone to such an extent that permanent injuries are of daily occurrence. We repeat from Plato, "Only the right combination of both mental and physical culture makes the soul circumspect and manly."

This should likewise be observed by invalids suffering from chronic diseases; impatience or the desire to force and precipitate the desired results being often injurious and contrary to the rules of nature.

We will, at all times and under all circumstances, be accessible to physicians, to patients, persons of inactive habits, parents, and teachers, to make intelligible individualized gymnastics, calculated to cure many indispositions and diseases, to prevent the same, to develop the growing body to strength and robust health, and retain health and vigor up to the highest age.

PART II.

Hydro-Therapeutics and Their Relation to Gymnastics; or, Vinzenz Prisznitz[1] and Peter Henry Ling.

WHEN, after the invention and discoveries of Vinzenz Prisznitz, water in its different temperatures, in its various forms of application, was recognized as a powerful and valuable agency, in not only relieving and curing chronic diseases, but also in controlling and subduing acute disorders; when these valuable discoveries had attracted the attention of the scientific world and received the sanction and encouragement of the government (Austria), they were greeted with joy by the chronically afflicted half of the human race, and soon became formulated into a new system of the healing art.

Prisznitz, during the first period of his triumph (he had then from 500 to 600 patients all the year round), favored low temperatures, and the time of different baths prescribed was frequently of considerable duration, making it necessary, in

---

[1] No name in medical literature, during the last half of our present century, has suffered more misspelling than that of this celebrated man; we give it here in the original; his individual signature was uniformly V. Prisznitz.

order to secure a complete reaction, to subject his patients to a great amount of physical exertion immediately after such baths. *Long walks* and *wood-sawing* were his favorite exercises. It was about this time (1840 to 1845) that the name of that new apostle and reformer became known, Peter Henry Ling, "the inventor of a new system of movements for the development of the healthy body and for the cure of many diseases, Professor at Stockholm, Knight of the North Star, Member of the Royal Swedish Academy of Sciences," etc.

His writings, and the practical illustrations of them, created fresh interest in Physical Culture and in Medical Gymnastics everywhere, and, covering a larger field in their variety of purpose than any other system known, soon found their way into all grades of society of every nation.

They included an especial division for the training of the military, and were early translated into German, English, French, Italian, etc. (Into German in 1846 by Dr. Maaszman, of Magdeburg.) And their merits having been thoroughly and technically investigated by orders of the different governments, these *Military Gymnastics* to this day form a very essential part in the training of young soldiers in all the armies of Europe.

Even conservative Russia became mindful of their great importance, and when it was proposed

that a M. De Ron, who had been a disciple of
Ling, and had introduced this system· at the
Russian capital, should be decorated with the
"Order of St. Anne," the Emperor wished a
detailed report regarding De Ron's merits, as well
as regarding Ling's system, in consequence of
which the Supreme Medical Board of the Empire
presented two reports, of which the following
brief extracts were taken from a legalized copy of
the official documents:

"The inquiry into the merits of the Institution
of M. De Ron was confided to two members of the
Medical Council, Spaski and Ligorski. In their
report they state that notwithstanding M. Spaski
had frequented this institution as a patient during
four months of 1847, and, of course, had an
opportunity of experiencing the effect of the
treatment by movements, and of becoming
acquainted with the usefulness of the method,
they still considered it their special duty to study
it carefully by frequent visits and impartially
examining the treatment employed in different
diseases.

"The following is the result of their careful
observation: Notwithstanding bodily exercises,
under the name of 'Turnen,' were generally known
and practiced in Germany at the beginning of the
present century, and many of its enlightened

professional as well as non-professional writers tried to give to the 'Turnen' a rational direction, by combining it with anatomy and physiology, Ling must be considered as the founder of the rational system of movements, since in his establishment not only the theory and practice of movements, but also a perfect knowledge of anatomy and physiology was considered to be the indispensable basis of his system."

Again: "Experience teaches us the usefulness of this institution, as many persons treated by movements have recovered their health, after having suffered from diseases which could not be cured by the ordinary remedies."

"From the foregoing facts, the Medical Council has come to the conclusion that the activity and practice of M. De Ron, the founder of the first establishment in Russia for the cure of diseases by movements, in which many persons have completely recovered their health, or have obtained substantial relief, by means of that important therapeutic accessory, deserve all encouragement from the Government."

"At the present time, all learned men agree that bodily exercises, methodically practiced, are necessary to every one from childhood, in order to develop regularly the strength of the body and to promote robust health. The practice of these movements is of the greatest importance for those who are in the public service, in which a robust, agile, and well-trained body is required, in order to undergo the fatigues of military life," etc., etc. Signed—*Dr. Markus*, President of the Medical Department, and eleven gentlemen, consulting members of the Medical Council.

Both these men were without any special medical education. Prisznitz was a farmer, a peasant, and his mental attainments such as could be procured at country public schools of those days. But he was a man of a clear mind, of a firm will, gifted with wonderful natural ingenuity and instinctive promptings, entirely honest and sincere. Yet, while we admit that he stands to-day in history as the hero of modern hydro-therapeutics, illustrious for his courage to struggle successfully against the superstitions and credulities of a thousand years, he was not their supreme master who brought that system to a consummate perfection. We celebrate Christopher Columbus as the discoverer of America, yet he saw but a very small part of this great country.

To Peter Henry Ling then, undoubtedly, we must give at least the credit of having furnished the keystone to the grand structure erected by Prisznitz. It is more than the keystone; it is, in fact, the most essential and strongest pillar of

3

support, to forever uphold that great temple of
nature's self-salvation, plainly and popularly
called "Water Cure."

Prisznitz represents the Romans and their love
for baths, defining and improving the healing
virtues of them, increasing and modifying their
forms of application for the benefit of suffering
humanity; Ling representing Greece in her
palmiest days of physical culture and health-
giving exercises, offering strength and corporal
beauty to all who follow him. Wherever the
forces discovered and developed by them may
join, they must conquer.

Peter Henry Ling was a man of scholarly
inclinations; he had traveled extensively, mastering
four or five languages, had passed successfully
theological examinations and became afterward
private tutor in some of the best families at
Stockholm. But he was of a restless and impet-
uous nature. In 1801 he took part in the sea-
fight against Nelson, as a volunteer in the Danish
Navy. He received at various times military
appointments, acquitting himself creditably in
every sphere. The same impulsive energy led
him to study the art of fencing. Two fencing-
masters, French refugees, had founded at
Stockholm a fencing-school. Ling was there
every day, and his great skill in this art was soon

generally acknowledged. The more skillful he became, the more he valued it. His reflection upon fencing, and his personal experience, and beneficial results (for he suffered then from gout, the sequel of reckless exposure), taught him to appreciate the wholesome effects which may be produced on the body, as well as the mind, by movements based on rational principles, a circumstance that suggested to him a new and elevated idea, the full development of which could not be accomplished by fencing only.

This idea was, that an harmonious organic development of the body, and of its powers and capabilities, by well-systematized exercises, considered in relation to the organic and intellectual faculties, may constitute an essential part in the general education of a people.

The realization of this idea now became his grand aim, the more so as he pictured to himself the brilliant image of mankind restored to health, strength, and beauty. Ling thought not, like some of his predecessors, of merely imitating the gymnastic treatment of the ancients, but he aimed at its entire reformation and improvement.

In the year 1826 the well-known authoress, Mrs. Ehrenstroem, wrote: "Sweden will never be able to acknowledge all it owes to the art of Ling." She might have said this of the world at large.

Unlike Ling, Vinzenz Prisznitz never left his native hills, but, similar to the experience of Ling, his great discoveries were made mostly during experiments and watchful observations on his own person during a very painful situation. He had met with a serious accident, being thrown from a spirited horse, fracturing two ribs, having his face and arm terribly lacerated by the shoes of the beast, and receiving other injuries, distressing and dangerous besides. He had no confidence in the doctors of his immediate neighborhood; in fact, they had pronounced him beyond recovery, but he trusted to cold water as a safe anti-phlogistic, and to generous nature's own restorative virtues, and thus, after a few weeks, remaining in a restful position, applying cool compresses and baths in various forms, was rewarded by regaining his health, and soon thereafter a perfect recovery from all his injuries.

He was then only 19 years of age, but although, as we believe, he had never seen, or possessed, a copy of Shakespeare, acted strictly upon the sentiments of Macbeth:

"Throw physic to the dogs; I'll none of it!

And from this time forward his name and, with it, his reputation as a man of genius spread far and wide and to the remotest parts of the globe. In the year 1830 his patients numbered but forty-five. In the year 1840 they had increased to over fifteen hundred. He had to put up building after building for their accommodation. They crowded in from all parts of the world; among them princes, men of nobility, and many leading men of the medical profession.

In this country the first hydro-therapeutic institute was opened at Brattleboro, Vermont, in the year 1845, under the able direction of Dr. Robert Wesselhoeft, associated soon thereafter with Dr. Charles W. Grau, a gentleman of fine attainments and scholarly ability.

The employment of various exercises, systematized for the proper development of the human body, as well as for the cure of diseases, was known in the most ancient times. If we go back to the mythological era, we find that Æsculapius was thought to have been the inventor of these movements, and we are told that Medea recommended them for the purpose of giving vigor to weakly persons. Iccus of Tarentum and Herodicus of Selymbra gave them a scientific basis. The last made use of them for medical purposes, which may be the reason that he is considered to have been the original inventor of this art. Hippocrates, as previously stated, was one of his pupils, superintending the exercises in his "palaestra." Galen, Cornelius, Celsus, Avicenna and Oribasius have recommended in their writings the free use of these exercises. Mercuriale wrote a treatise in the year 1569, "De Arte Gymnastica," in which he recorded the most important exercises used by the Greeks and Romans. Among the writers of the last and present century, we quote Hoffman, Stahl, Fisher, Albertus, Boerner, Gerike, and Heiter. In the year 1728 Francis Fuller, a surgeon in London, wrote a treatise which he called "Medicina Gymnastica," and in which he strongly recommends certain movements in various diseases, according to the example of the great Sydenham. In 1780 Tissot published a work on Gymnastics, which induced several progressive medical men to employ those means with great satisfaction. In 1794 John Pugh, the anatomist, published "a physiological, theoretical, and practical treatise on the utility of scientific muscular action for restoring the physical powers."

Londe wrote, about sixty years ago, an interesting work, entitled "Gymnastique Médicale." We believe he was the first to foresee the importance of applying specific movements to specific circumstances of different cases. The realization of this idea, however, was reserved for Ling's genius.

On the use of single and principally passive movements, resistive and mixed movements,

vibratious, percussion, and compression, in different diseases, there are many excellent works. We
have no less than twenty-five treatises on friction
alone. Of late years, the French have taken up
the more gentle part of passive movements, such
as kneading, pressing, rubbing, pinching, etc.,
applied by expert manipulators, and have called
them "Massage."

"Dr. Douglas Graham, of Boston, in his late
"Treatise on Massage,"[1] a very valuable and comprehensive work on the subject, ventures to
give the French credit for having systematized
and made use of these movements under that
name, and states that the term *massage* has
appeared in their medical literature during the
last sixty years, while Dr. M. Roth, of London,
in his work on "Medical Gymnastics,"[2] states
that "several years ago, Prof. Georgii endeavored
to make this method known at Paris, by the
publication of his "Kinesitherapia," and by
showing practically the beneficial results of these
movements in the treatment of diseases. The
Minister of Public Instruction, Salvandy, had
already made, some years previously, preliminary
arrangements for introducing Ling's doctrine into
France, but these were put a stop to by the late
French revolution [1848].'

[1] Vail & Co., publishers, 1890.
[2] 1856, p. 23.

This "Massage," according to Dr. Graham's own definitions, however, is nothing but a subdivision of Ling's system, and if Prof. Billroth, of Vienna, or Dr. Wagener, of probably Freiburg (not Friedburg), had been interrogated or consulted on Swedish movements in place of "Massage," there would have been less perplexity regarding their therapeutic acknowledgement, their popular applications, and their proper origin in the sayings and writings of those gentlemen.

Ling's works were not translated into French until the year 1845, and if any part of his system had been practiced in France previous to that time, it very likely partook of the character Dr. Graham refers to when speaking of Moltenot, who masséed at Orleans in 1833,—an empiric. This kind of "massage" has been in vogue with the applications of Russian and Turkish baths since the dawn of the nineteenth century in all parts of Europe, and was known long before Ling ever published any writings regarding his own system. That all therapeutic gymnastics and medical movements are of very ancient origin—"hoary with antiquity," as Dr. Graham forcibly expresses it, has not been contradicted by Ling; but to him belongs the credit of never having imitated the ancients and of having developed, with scientific and practical clearness, a compact system of his own, with a larger range of usefulness for medical purposes than any system known in modern times.

That part of it which may have been appropriated and incorporated under the old name of Massage, has been practiced as Ling's system in Germany for many years. These light and passive movements and diverse manipulations are highly valued by progressive gynæcologists for their efficacy in treating prolapsus, displacements, and many other uterine disorders, and by neurologists in hysteria, and for their salutary effects in stimulating the nutritive and assimilative organs to increased healthful action. Hence, "Fat and Blood, and How to Make Them," as presented in a work by Dr. Mitchell, of Philadelphia. This coincides with the views of De Ron, St. Petersburg; of A. C. Newman, Leipzig; E. G. Ravenstein, London; Major Rothstein, Berlin; Prof. Richter, Dresden, and M. Roth, of London, as can be traced in their numerous publications. It is also a well-known fact that Stockholm, capital of Sweden, has, since Ling's first triumphs there, been looked upon as, and is considered this day, the "Mecca for Gynæcologists." The Central Institute, now under Prof. Toerngren, and the establishment of Major Thure Brandt, are very successful in the treatment of pelvic affections, and attract their patients, as Prisznitz and Graefenberg in former years, from every quarter of the globe. Of Major Brandt it is said that his knowledge of pelvic anatomy is not excelled by any medical practitioner on either side of the Atlantic.

Prof. Playfair, with all his light-heartedness regarding the intelligence and practical skill of his manipulators (*masseurs*), and his readiness to change them whenever he considers it advisable, stands to-day as the most successful expounder of the system *in general practice*. His case of tubercular peritonitis and its cure, as described by Dr. T. Lauder Brunton in one of his "Lettsomian Lectures" (1884), is next to miraculous. This is probably the case Dr. Graham has recorded through an error, as having been under treatment of Dr. T. Lauder Branton (misprint for Brunton), p. 162. This patient, by request of Dr. Brunton, was treated by Prof. Playfair. All this shows the great importance of regulated muscular actions for medical purposes, to which, we are convinced, a great part of the results produced by modern hydro-therapeutics is owing, in which the douche, the compress, the wet-sheet pack, the regular frictions, etc., have such a marked influence. Our impartial reflection, then, must lead us to the conclusion that a complete combination of these two disciplines presents itself as a natural ultimatum. This view has been fully recognized by the leading institutions on both sides of the ocean. The doctrines of Prisznitz and. of Ling were both inspired by a pious confidence in the infinite love and wisdom of nature. They have vindicated her ways. They should be inseparable, in order to thus eventually redeem mankind from nine-tenths of its physical misery.

While Russia, through her government, may be named as one of the pioneers in adopting, encouraging, and following the system and philosophy of Ling, strange to state, she has been slow and hesitating to appreciate the discoveries of Prisznitz. A large number of private institutions have been opened and are successfully conducted within her territory; yet, while Austria and other governments had sent their best and most noted medical men, one of them the Imperial "Sanitäts-Rath" Baron von Turkheim, to Graefenberg, to investigate Prisznitz and the merits of his new system; while their reports were most favorable, so as to place the Graefenberg Institute under government protection, while Prussia, and, through the agency of her military supremacy, all Germany have adopted some important parts of hydro-therapeutics into their field surgery, reducing amputations almost fifty per cent.; while the best results in the treatment of fevers, especially typhoid, are recorded everywhere, the London *Lancet*, one of the leading medical journals of England, in one of its late publications (July, 1891), brings a copy of a report—semi-official—by Dr. Kurkutoff, from which the following extract is here inserted: "We have examined the physiological effects of baths administered to typhoid-fever patients at Prof. Manascin's clinic, in St. Petersburg, and find that such baths exert only a slight effect on the assimilation of the fatty constituents of foods, which, as in other fevers, is notably less than in healthy persons, and indeed varies directly with the gravity of the case. But there seems to be a good deal of difference as to the power of assimilation of fatty matter in different cases, probably depending on the functional disturbance in the bowels and on the amount of the individual peculiarities of the patient. In the graver cases the effect of the bath was to improve somewhat the assimilation of fat to the average extent of nearly four per cent.," etc. The London *Lancet* quotes Dr. Kurkutoff complete, including his "individual peculiarities," and seems to assimilate the "fatty constituents" without noticing much confusion, or his great haste to carry matters to a point. It brings the report without comment.

To us it appears to be a labored effort, more to avoid a fair examination than to face such honest facts as might have been discovered, had Dr. Kurkutoff felt at all inclined or anxious to investigate.

> "Of course! But only shun too sharp a tension,
> For just where fails the comprehension,
> A word steps promptly in as deputy.
> With words 't is excellent disputing;
> Systems to words 't is easy suiting,
> On words 't is convenient believing,
> No word can ever lose a jot from thieving."
> —MEPHISTO.

In this country, the Brattleboro Institute must certainly be credited with having first recognized the great importance of incorporating the system of Ling into their field of action, of considering the discoveries of Prisznitz and the system of Ling one, and combining the virtues and efficacy of baths, pure mountain air, soft spring water, properly regulated diet, etc., with those of wholesome and well-defined exercises. Others have since followed, and at present no sanitarium of hydro-therapeutic tendencies is considered complete without this combination.

PRISZNITZ HIMSELF.

In the year 1843 Captain R. T. Claridge, of England, published a small volume on "Hydro-therapy, or the Cold Water Cure," as practiced by Vinzenz Prisznitz, at Graefenberg. Five editions, the first three of one thousand each, followed by two editions of two thousand each, were sold in less than ten months. He presented partly his own individual experience, partly that of prominent German writers, who first diffused a knowledge of Prisznitz and his system all over Europe. His admiration of this distinguished man is partly a just return for the recovery of his own health, as he had traveled for a number of years, visiting and consulting every celebrated physician in Europe without finding relief; partly an expression of feelings that everybody experiences when brought in contact with a man of superior genius. Such was the power of Prisznitz, the great reformer of medical science, that nobody who approached him could help coming under his influence. As a layman in medicine, Captain Claridge did not find any difficulty or doubt, as physicians frequently did, when considering how Prisznitz operated, and comparing their professional wisdom with his simple doings. He followed merely the hints of nature, which, although hidden as they may be in their last principles, were clear enough to the unprejudiced eye. It is most interesting to read now what Captain Claridge said about this remarkable man.

"He [Prisznitz] is a man of deep reflection, and

of few words, for he says but little at a time and
rarely promises anything; consequently, his words
when spoken are considered as sacred, by high
and low, as the responses of the Delphic Oracle.
Many people complain that he does not talk
enough, and doctors who come here to learn the
treatment say that he never explains anything to
them. With respect to the first allegation, it
must be evident that a man who has all the year
round from 500 to 1000 patients, besides the
peasantry of the neighborhood that may require
his aid, cannot have a great deal of breath to
throw away. Let any person speak to him on his
own or his family's case, and he will find his reply
that of a man of profound sense, a reply that he,
Prisznitz, never wishes to retract, and for which
he will give his reasons in the most unaffected
manner possible. But with respect to the second
complaint, it must be avowed that he has no very
great regard for medical men of the old school,
because no one has suffered more from their
vindictive feelings than himself; besides, he has
ever found it a work of supererogation to endeavor
to dispossess them of their prejudices; nor has he
time or inclination to enter into disputes upon a
mode of treatment which he knows, as directly
emanating from nature, to be always true to itself.
He has frequently witnessed the conduct of

medical men who came to inquire into the mode of treatment, who took a carriage at Freiwaldau, went up to Graefenberg, looked at the baths, the douches, rooms, etc., and proceeded home to decry a discovery, of the merits of which they knew nothing.

'That Prisznitz has founded some sort of theory on this mode of treatment, after so many years of successful practice, and with the help of that inquiring genius, and that natural, impenetrable calmness which so particularly distinguishes him, there can be little doubt. And this theory has never failed him in his treatment of the most complicated diseases. But he has no time for writing; and if he had, he would find it extremely difficult to explain himself, since it is an extraordinary fact that no two cases are treated exactly alike. There is no doubt that Prisznitz owes all his experience to his utter ignorance of "Medical Science," which indeed, is his greatest advantage; for what really does the history of medicine offer but the discouraging picture of the instability of principles and a series of theories succeeding each other, without any one of them being able to content an upright spirit, or satisfy an inquiring mind.

"We can hardly expect, however, that Prisznitz will ever attempt to give the world any medical or

systematic details. This is left to literary persons
or young medical men, who should observe all
that is observable, and communicate their observations, so as to formulate a whole of that which
is most important. Fortune and fame will be the
reward of any of our honest students who may go
to Graefenberg and thoroughly study the
proceedings of this extraordinary man.

"To do this effectually, they must be possessed of
patience, as it can only be studied on the spot.
Nothing but danger would result from acting on
the dictation of books, as will be illustrated by
the following case, whilst the author was at
Graefenberg: A person who had lost his wife
and two children, was attacked with brain fever.
Prisznitz ordered him a tepid bath, in which he
sat, and was rubbed by two men, who were
occasionally changed. The patient became so
deranged that it was with difficulty he could be
kept in the bath. In ordinary cases this disease
succumbs to the treatment in two or three hours;
but the man in this case became speechless at the
end of this time. Prisznitz, with that coolness
which is so leading a feature in his character,
said: "Keep on, until he either talks much or goes
to sleep." The latter the man at last did, but not
until he had been in the bath for nine hours and a
half; that is to say, they commenced with him at

4

one o'clock in the day, and the patient fell asleep
from exhaustion at half-past ten at night.   He was
then put to bed, and next day the fever had left
him, and though weak, he was able to walk about.
A similar case had not occurred at Graefenberg
for nearly three years.   This shows the difficulty
of anyone practicing who has not well studied
the technics of the cure.   If the practitioner had
become alarmed after the first two or three hours,
and had ordered the patient out of the bath to
change the treatment, the consequences might
have proved fatal.

"Many medical men have been at Graefenberg,
some on their own account, and others on that of
their respective governments, who, after a
residence of three or four months, went away
imagining that they were as great or greater
professors of the new science than Prisznitz, and
that they perfectly understood the system.   On
arriving at home they have opened institutions,
and Graefenberg exhibits at this moment many
melancholy proofs of their ignorance of even the
first principles of the science.   The mere application of water, in its variety of forms and
temperatures, appears so simple, that one
constantly hears people, who do not even
understand the composition of that element,
pretend that, when they arrive at home, they may

be perfectly able to doctor themselves and their friends. But this will be found a dangerous experiment."

We think nobody will read this extract of Captain Claridge, in connection with some other chapters of this volume, without feeling as if a weight of heavy fetters had been removed from his limbs. The whole high-built system of medicine, the tyrannical treatment, with its horrible tortures, of the old drug system, its assumed wisdom and inflated nonsense, fall like a mist before his eyes, and the use of drugs, patent medicines, plasters, blisters, etc., stands annihilated before him.

When we bear in mind that all diseases are but the legitimate result of false conditions, such as living in bad air, poorly ventilated rooms, eating too rich or unwholesome food, using narcotics, and stimulants, taking irritant poisons, abstaining from healthful exercise, etc., we must see at once that forsaking all these unnatural habits and returning to the normal and more natural conditions, must, if anything can, result in the restoration of health. Restoring people thus to the natural state of living is an essential element in the practice of every judicious hydro-therapeutist. We know it may be said that the truly great and intuitive Prisznitz did not pay very much regard to the diet of his patients; but that only proves that the other conditions he observed were true to health, as, in spite of this deviation, hundreds, nay, thousands, of the worst cases, which had baffled the skill of the world's best surgeons and physicians, were cured with ease and certainty. And again, though Prisznitz seems to have been inspired, as it were, with powers divine, to perform such miraculous cures, yet there is no intelligent mind but must perceive that he would have succeeded much more surely if he had been more acquainted with anatomy, physiology, and pathology of the human system.

We come now to the last strong testimony in favor of our great physician—Nature. It is that of a man known in every civilized country. His name is Sir Bulwer Lytton.

The reader will notice that he has to be doubly thankful to the little book of Captain Claridge, as Sir Lytton acknowledges that it was not until he saw it that his attention was drawn to the new system of the healing art. We will readily be pardoned for presenting a copious extract from Sir Lytton's letter. Although it was written (for the *New Monthly Magazine*, London,) several years ago, it will never lose its luster nor its charm:

" And freed from the fumes of a lore-cramped brain,
Bathe in thy dew and be well again.

Here we are, Mr. Editor, in these days of cant and jargon, preaching up the education of the mind, forcing our children under melon-frames, and babbling to the laborer and mechanic, 'Read and read and read,' as if God had not given us muscles, and nerves, and bodies, subjected to exquisite pains as pleasures—as if the body were not to be cared for and cultivated, as well as the mind; as if health were no blessing, instead of that capital good without which all other blessings—save the hope of health eternal—grow flat and joyless; as if the enjoyment of the world in which we are, was not more closely linked with our physical than our mental selves, so long as our nerves are jaded and prostrate, our senses dim and heavy, our relationship with nature abridged and thwarted by the jaundiced eye, and failing limb, and trembling hand—the apothecary's shop between us and the sun! For the mind, we admit that to render it strong and clear, habit and discipline are required; how deal we, especially we, Mr. Editor, of the London world, we of the literary craft,—we of the restless, striving brotherhood,—how deal we with the body? We carry it on with us as a post horse, from stage to stage. Does it flag? No rest! give it rein or the spur. We begin to feel the frame break under us. We administer a drug, gain a temporary relief, shift the disorder from one part to another, forget our ailments in our excitements, and when we pause at last, thoroughly shattered, with complaints grown chronic, diseases fastened to the organs, send for the doctors in good earnest, and die as your predecessors and your rival died, under combinations of long neglected maladies, which could never have been known had we done for the body what we do for the mind—made it strong by discipline, and maintained it firm by habit.

"Not alone calling to recollection our departed friends, but looking over the vast field of suffering which those acquainted with the lives of men who think and labor cannot fail to behold around them, I confess, though I have something of Canning's disdain of professed philanthropists, and do not love every knife grinder as much as if he were my brother—I confess, nevertheless, that I am filled with an earnest pity; and an anxious desire seizes me to communicate to others the simple process of healing and well-being which has passed under my own experience, and to which I gratefully owe days no longer weary of the sun, and nights which no longer yearn for and dread the morrow.

"And now, Mr. Editor, I may be pardoned, I trust, if I illustrate by my own case the system I commend to others.

"I have been a workman in my day. I began to write, and to toil, and to win some kind of a name, which I had the ambition to improve, while yet little more than a boy. With strong love for study in books, with yet greater desire to accomplish myself in the knowledge of men, for sixteen years I can conceive no life to have been more filled by occupation than mine. What time was not given to action was given to study; what time not given to study, to action—labor in both! To a constitution naturally far from strong, I allowed no pause or respite. The wear and tear went on without intermission, the whirl of the wheel never ceased. Sometimes, indeed, thoroughly overpowered and exhausted, I sought for escape. The physicians said 'Travel,' and I traveled; 'Go into the country,' and I went. But in such attempts at repose all my ailments gathered round me, made themselves far more palpable and felt. I had no resource but to fly from myself—to fly into the other world of books, or thought, or reverie; to live in some state of being less painful than my own. As long as I was always at work, it seemed that I had no leisure to be ill. Quiet was my hell.

"At length, the frame thus long neglected, patched up for awhile by drugs and doctors, put off and trifled with as an intrusive dun, like a dun who is in his rights, brought in its arrears, crushing and terrible, accumulated through many years. Worn out and wasted, the constitution seemed wholly inadequate to meet the demand. The exhaustion of toil and study had been completed by great anxiety and grief. I had watched with alternate hope and fear the lingering and mournful death-bed of my nearest relation and dearest friend—of the persons around whom was entwined the strongest affection my life had known; and when all was over, I seemed scarcely to live myself.

"At this time I was thoroughly shattered. The least attempt at exercise exhausted me. The nerves gave way at the most ordinary excitement. A chronic irritation of that vast surface we call the mucous membrane, which had defied for years all medical skill, rendered me continually liable to acute attacks, which, from their repetition and increased feebleness of my frame, might at any time be fatal. My sleep was without refreshment. At morning I rose more weary than I lay down to rest. Without fatiguing you and your readers further with the *longa cohors* of my complaints, I pass on to record my struggle to resist them. I have always had a great belief in the power of the will. What a man determines to do, that in ninety-nine cases out of the

hundred, I hold that he succeeds in doing. I
determined to have insight into a knowledge I
had never attained since manhood—the knowledge
of health.

"I resolutely put away books and study, sought
the airs which the physicians esteemed the most
healthful, and adopted the strict regimen on
which all the children of Æsculapius so wisely
insist. In short, I maintained the same general
habits as to hours, diet (with the exception of
wine, which, in moderate quantities, seemed to me
indispensable), and, so far as my strength would
allow, of exercise, as I found afterwards instituted
at hydro-therapeutic establishments. I dwell on
this to forestall, in some manner, the common
remark of persons not well acquainted with the
medical agencies of water; that it is to the
regular life which patients, under this discipline,
lead, and not to the element itself, and alone, that
they owe their recovery. Nevertheless, I found
that these changes, however salutary in theory,
produced little, if any, practical amelioration in
my health. All invalids know, perhaps, how
difficult, under ordinary circumstances, is the
alteration of habits from bad to good. The early
rising, the walk before breakfast, so delicious in
the feelings of freshness and vigor which they
bestow upon the strong, often become punishments

to the invalid. Headache, languor, a sense of weariness over the eyes, a sinking of the whole system towards noon, which seemed imperiously to demand the dangerous aid of stimulants, was all I obtained by the morning breeze, and the languid stroll by the seashore. The suspension from study afflicted me with intolerable *ennui*, and added to the profound dejection of the spirits. The brain, so long accustomed to morbid activity, was but withdrawn from its usual occupations to invent horrors and chimeras. Over the pillow, vainly sought two hours before midnight, hovered no golden sleep. The absence of excitement, however unhealthy, only aggravated the symptoms of ill health.

"It was at this time that I met, by chance, in the library at St. Leonhard's, with Captain Claridge's work on the 'Water Cure,' as practiced by Prisznitz, at Graefenberg. Making allowance for certain exaggerations therein, which appeared evident to my common sense, enough still remained not only to captivate the imagination and flatter the hopes of an invalid, but to appeal with favor to his sober judgment. Till then perfectly ignorant of the subject and the system, except by some such vague stories and good jests as had reached my ears in Germany, I resolved at least to read what more could be said in favor of the *ariston udor*, and examine dispassionately into its merits as a medicament. I was then under the advice of one of the first physicians of our age. I had consulted half the faculty. I had every reason to be grateful for the attention, and to be confident in the skill, of those whose prescriptions had, from time to time, flattered my hopes and enriched the chemist. But the truth must be spoken; far from being better, I was sinking fast, little remaining to me to try in the great volume of the herbal.

"Seek what I would next, even if a quackery, it certainly might expedite my grave, but it could scarcely render life—at least the external life—more unjoyous. Accordingly, I examined, with such grave thoughts as a sick man brings to bear upon his case, all the grounds upon which to justify to myself an excursion to the snows of Silesia. But I own, that in proportion as I found my faith in the system strengthen, I shrunk from the terrors of this long journey to the rugged region in which the probable lodging would be a laborer's cottage,[1] and in which the babel of a

---

[1] Let me not disparage the fountain-head of the "Water Cure," the parent institution of the great Prisznitz. I believe many of the earlier hardships complained of at Graefenberg have been removed or amended, and such as remain, are no doubt well compensated by the vast experience and extraordinary tact of a man who will rank hereafter among the most illustrious discoverers who have ever benefited the human race.

hundred languages, so agreeable to the healthful delight in novelty, so appalling to the sickly despondency of the hypochondriac, would murmur and growl over a public table spread with no tempting condiments. Could I hope to find healing in my own land, and not too far from my own physicians in case of failure, I might indeed solicit the water-gods. But that journey! I, who scarcely lived through a day without leeches or pills; the long, gelid journey to Graefenberg; I should be sure to fall ill by the way, to be clutched and mismanaged by some German doctor, depositing my bones in some dismal churchyard on the banks of the Father Rhine.

"While thus perplexed, I fell in with one of the pamphlets written by Dr. Wilson, of Malvern, and my doubts were solved. Here was an English physician who had himself known more than my own sufferings; who, like myself, had found the pharmacopœia in vain, who had spent ten months at Graefenberg, and left all his complaints behind him; who, fraught with the experience he had acquired, not only in his own person, but from scientific examination of cases under his eye, had transported the system to our native shores, and who proffered the proverbial salubrity of Malvern air, and its holy springs, to those who, like me, had ranged in vain, from simple to mineral, and who had become bold by despair; bold enough to try if health, like truth, lay at the bottom of a well. I was not then aware that other institutions had been established in England, of more or less fame. I saw in Dr. Wilson the first transporter, at least as a physician, of the Silesian system, and did not pause to look out for other and later pupils of this innovating German school.

"I resolved then to betake myself to Malvern. On my way through the city, I paused, in the innocence of my heart, to inquire of the faculty if they thought the 'Water Cure' would suit my case. With one exception, they were unanimous in the vehemence of their denunciations. Granting, even, that in some cases, especially of rheumatism, that system had produced a cure, to my complaints it was worse than inapplicable; it was highly dangerous; it would probably be fatal. I had no stamina for the treatment; it would fix chronic ailments into organic disease; sure, it would be much better to try what I had not yet tried. 'What I had not yet tried?' A course of prussic acid! Nothing was better for gastric irritation, which was no doubt the main cause of my sufferings! If, however, I were obstinately bent upon so mad an experiment, Dr. Wilson was the last person I should go to. I was not deterred by all these intimidations, nor seduced by the salubrious allurements of the prussic acid under its scientific appellation of hydrocyanic. A little reflection taught me that the members of a learned profession are naturally the very persons least disposed to favor innovation upon the practices which custom and prescription have rendered sacred in their eyes. An old-school physician can scarcely be expected to own that a Silesian peasant will cure with simple water the diseases which resist his armament of phials. And with regard to the peculiar objection to Dr. Wilson, I had read in his own pamphlets attacks upon the orthodox practice sufficient to account for, perhaps to justify, the disposition to depreciate him in return. Still, my friends were anxious and fearful; to please them I continued to inquire, though not of physicians, but of patients. I sought out some of those who had gone through the process. I sifted some of the cases of cure cited by Dr. Wilson. I found the account of such patients so encouraging, the cases quoted so authentic, that I grew impatient of delay. I threw physic to the dogs, and went to Malvern.

"It is not my intention, Mr. Editor, to detail the course I underwent. The different resources of water, as a medicament, are to be found in many works easily to be obtained, and well worth the study. In this letter I suppose myself to be addressing those as thoroughly acquainted with the system as I, myself, was at the first, and I deal, therefore, only in generals.

"The first point which impressed and struck me was the extreme and utter innocence of the new system in skillful hands. Certainly when I went, I believed it to be a kill or cure affair. I fancied it must be a violent remedy, that it doubtless might effect great and magical cures, but that if it failed, it might be fatal. Now, I speak not alone of my own case, but of the immense number of cases I have seen—patients of all ages, all species and genera of diseases, all kinds and conditions of constitutions, when I declare, upon my honor, that I never witnessed one dangerous symptom produced by the 'Water Cure,' whether at Dr. Wilson's, or other institutions which I afterwards visited. And though unquestionably fatal consequences might occur from gross mismanagement, and as unquestionably have so occurred at various establishments, I am yet convinced that water in its constituents is so friendly to the human body, that it requires a very extraordinary degree of bungling, of ignorance, and presumption, to produce results really dangerous; that a so-called regular practitioner does more frequent mischief from the misapplication of even the simplest drugs, than a hydro-therapeutic physician of moderate experience does, or can do, by the misapplication of his baths, friction, etc. And here I must observe, that those portions of the treatment which appear to the uninitiated as the most perilous, are really the safest, such as the wet-sheet-packing, and can be applied with the most impunity to the weakest constitution; whereas, those which appear, from our greater familiarity with them, the least startling and most innocuous, the plunge-bath, the douche, are those which require the greatest care and a knowledge of general pathology of the individual constitution.

"The next thing that struck me was the extraordinary ease with which, under this system, good habits are acquired and bad habits relinquished. The difficulty with which, under orthodox medical treatment, stimulants are abandoned, is here not witnessed. Patients accustomed for a half century to live hard and high, wine-drinkers, spirit-bibbers, whom the old school physician has sought in vain to reduce to a daily pint of sherry, here voluntarily resign strong potations, after a day or two cease to feel the want of them, and reconcile themselves to water, as if they had drank nothing else all their lives. Others who have had recourse for years to medicine—their potion in the morning, their cordial at noon, their pill before dinner, their narcotic at bedtime—cease to require these aids to life, as if by charm. Nor this alone. Men to whom mental labor has been a necessity, who have existed on the excitement of the passions and the stir of the intellect, who have felt, with these withdrawn, the prostration of the whole system,—the block to the wheel of the entire machine,—return at once to the careless spirits of the boy in his first holiday.

"Here lies the great secret. Water, thus skillfully administered, is in itself a wonderful excitement; it supplies the place of all others; it operates powerfully and rapidly upon the nerves, sometimes to calm them, sometimes to irritate, but always to occupy. Hence follows a consequence which all patients have observed: the complete repose of the passions during the early state of the cure; they seem.laid asleep as if by enchantment. The intellect shares the same rest; after a time, mental exertion becomes impossible; even the memory grows far less tenacious of its painful impressions; cares and griefs are forgotten; the sense of the present absorbs the past and future; there is a certain freshness and youth

5

which pervade the spirits and live upon the enjoyment of the actual hour. Thus, the great agents of moral wear and tear, the passions and the mind, are calmed into a strange rest. Nature seems to leave the body to its instinctive tendency, which is always towards recovery. All that interests and amuses is of a healthful character; exercise, instead of being an unwilling drudgery, becomes the inevitable impulse of the frame, braced and invigorated by the element. A series of reactions is always going on· the willing exercise produces refreshing rest. The extraordinary effect which water, taken early in the morning, produces on the appetite, is well known amongst those who have tried it, even before this new system was thought of. An appetite it should be the care of the skillful physician to check into moderate gratification; the powers of nutrition become singularly strengthened, the blood grows more rich and pure; the constitution is not only amended, it undergoes a change.

"(Dr. Wilson observed to me once, very truly, I think, that many old-school physicians are beginning to recognize the effect of water as a safe stimulant and a powerful anti-phlogistic, who yet do not perceive its far more complicated and beneficial effects in other directions.)

"The safety of the system, then, struck me first;

its power of replacing by healthful stimulants
the morbid ones it withdrew, whether physical
or moral, surprised me next; that which thirdly
impressed me was no less contrary to all my
preconceived notions. I had fancied that, whatever good or bad, the system must be one of great
hardship, extremely repugnant and disagreeable.
I wondered at myself to find how soon it became
so associated with pleasurable and grateful
feelings as to dwell upon the mind amongst the
happiest passages of existence. For my own part,
despite all my ailments, or whatever may have
been my cares, I have ever found exquisite
pleasure in that sense of being which is, as it
were, the conscience, the mirror of the soul. I
have known hours of as much, and as vivid,
happiness as, perhaps, can befall the lot of man,
but, amongst all my most brilliant recollections, I
can recall no periods of enjoyment at once more
hilarious and serene than the hours spent on the
lonely hills of Malvern—none in which nature was
so thoroughly possessed and appreciated. To rise
from a sleep sound as childhood's, the impatient
rush into the open air, while the sun was fresh,
the birds' first song, the sense of an unwonted
strength in every limb and nerve, which made so
light of the steep ascent to the holy spring, the
delicious sparkle of the morning draught, the

green terrace on the brow of the mountain, with
the rich landscape wide and below, the breeze
that once would have been so keen and biting,
now but arousing the blood and lifting the
spirits into religious joy; and keen sentiment of
present pleasure, rounded by a hope sanctioned
by all I felt in myself, and nearly all that I
witnessed in others, that that very present was
but the step, the threshold, into an unknown
and delightful region of health and vigor: disease
and care dropping from the frame and heart at
every stride.

"'To conclude my own case: I staid some nine
or ten weeks at Malvern, and business from
which I could not escape obliged me then to be
in the neighborhood of the city. I continued the
treatment seven weeks longer under Dr. Weiss, at
Petersham. . . . And now came, gradually, yet
perceptibly, the good effects of the system I had
undergone; flesh and weight returned, the sense
of health became conscious and steady; I had
every reason to bless the hour when I first sought
the springs of Malvern. And here I must
observe that it often happens that the patient, at
times, makes but slight apparent improvement
when under the cure, compared with that which
occurs subsequently. A hydro-therapeutic physician of repute, at Brussels, said frankly indeed

to a grumbling patient: 'I do not expect you
will be well while here; it is on leaving my
institution that you will know if I have cured you.'
It is as the frame recovers from the agitation it
undergoes, that it gathers round it powers utterly
unknown to it before; as the plant, watered by
the rains of one season, betrays in the next the
effect of the grateful showers.

"I had always suffered severely in winter;
the rigor of our last one gave me apprehensions,
and I resolved to seek shelter from my fears at
my beloved Malvern. I here passed the most
inclement period of the winter, not only perfectly
free from colds, rheums, and catarrhs, which had
heretofore visited me with the appearance of the
first snow, but in the enjoyment of excellent
health; and I am persuaded that for those who
are delicate, and whose sufferings increase during
the winter, there is no place where the cold is
so little felt as when under the gentle care and
shelter of a well-conducted hydro-therapeutic
institute. I am persuaded also, and in this I am
borne out by the experience of most physicians of
the new school, that consumption, in its earlier
stages, can be more easily cured, and the
predisposition more permanently eradicated
during fall and winter months at a good water-
cure, than by the timorous flight to Pisa, Madeira,

or other hot climes. It is by hardening, rather than defending and too carefully protecting, the tissues, that we best secure them from disease."

We will quote from the closing paragraph:

"And you, O parents! who, too indolent, too much slaves to custom, to endure the change for yourselves, to renounce for awhile your artificial natures, but who still covet for your children hardy constitutions, pure tastes, and abstemious habits; who wish to see them grow up with a manly disdain of luxury, with a vigorous indifference to climate, with a full sense of the value of health, not alone for itself, but for the powers it elicits and the virtues with which it is intimately connected; the serene, unfretful temper, the pleasures in innocent delight, the well-being that, content with self, expands in benevolence to others; you I adjure not to scorn the facile process of which I solicit the experiment. Dip your young heroes in the spring, and hold them not back by the heels. May my exhortations find believing listeners, and may some, now unknown to me, write me a word from the green hills of Malvern, or the groves of Petersham: 'We have harkened to you,—not in vain.' Adieu, Mr. Editor; the ghost returns to silence.

"E. BULWER LYTTON."

This article, so attractively written, so honestly and earnestly testifying in favor of hydro-therapeutics, was republished in many of our very best papers at the time. Had Sir Lytton lived to observe the progress which science has made since, closely combining the system of Ling with that of Prisznitz, and to speak of the great importance of this combination as demonstrated in every well-conducted hydro-therapeutic sanitarium of the present time, he would have sung its praise with still more enthusiasm; and his own recovery might have been accomplished with less sacrifice of time. We shall hereafter consider and deal with the two as one. Its philosophy represents all that is rational, according to the laws of nature, which are identical with the laws of health. Justus Liebig, the great scholar and chemist, late Baron von Liebig (for he was promoted to the privileges of nobility as a reward for his labors in the field of organic chemistry), was one of the most brilliant characters in the realms of science. The latest work he has placed before the world is his "Researches on the Chemistry of Food." He says: "I was induced to engage in a series of investigations which have led me further than I at first anticipated. The questions as to the nature of the organic acids diffused through our system, and that of the other substances contained therein, appeared to me so important to the right understanding and explanation of the vital processes, that I did not feel justified in proceeding with the revisal of my work until these questions had been, at least to a certain extent, experimentally answered."

These words show that Liebig is not the man to rest satisfied with work half done. We find him, too, following his old methods, for the first section of the book contains an examination of the order of investigation to be pursued in animal chemistry, and, as the first results, he finds that chemists have not devoted their energies to animal chemistry and physiology, and that both are "*frontier districts*," of which no one knows the exact limits.

"For centuries past," he continues, "men have endeavored to discover methods of cure or a knowledge of morbid conditions by the aid of imagination in the so-called systems of medicine; as if it were possible, or even wise and judicious, to expect a true insight into these things, or to look for intellectual illumination and progress from the most hazardous of *games of chance*.

"In modern times this method has been abandoned as entirely unproductive; but, on the other hand, men commit an error not less grave, inasmuch as, instead of acquiring by their own researches the knowledge necessary for the solution of their difficulties, they leave this duty to others, who, fully occupied with the cultivation of their own branches, have neither interest in the question to be solved, nor time or inclination for the task."

These are golden words. Nothing has reduced "Medical Science" so low in public estimation as the hypothetical systems that have been followed; systems whose basis and foundation have been the imagination, and not the experience, by careful observation. Is not this the state of medical practice now? Are we not blindly operating with our doses of drugs upon this or that disease, and this or that part of the system, without any knowledge or without certainty as to what chemical changes will be produced by drugs? Is not the treatment in hydro-therapeutic institutions constantly proving that we have nothing at last to cure but the *diseases produced by medicine?* Liberated from this burden, the system again develops its powers, the functions of the different organs are regularly performed once more, and the mind that so often succumbs under the weight of a diseased body, grows up again free and strong, governing life in a healthful and rational manner.

Perhaps the most important of all the incidental benefits to society from hydrotherapy is the check it is giving to quackery. The system itself, it was feared, would partake of this character. The founder of it, a peasant, without scientific training, was not the master to inspire confidence unconditionally; and it was to be feared that, in imitation of his example, some of his disciples might claim for their method the merit of a *great specialty*, or a *"cure-all,"* denouncing all other remedies as pernicious or useless. This fear has proved groundless. A few men of imperfect qualification did impose themselves on different communities as "water practitioners," but their sphere of operation was small and their practice of short duration. An establishment, with all necessary modern appliances, cannot be gotten up and attract patients without a considerable outlay of capital, and a medical superintendent of professional reputation. The very simplicity of the treatment is another safeguard against imposture. While it cannot be conducted with skill and safety in difficult cases, except by men of special training and medical culture, it offers to the impostor no mysteries with which to beguile the ignorant. But this is only a negative view of the subject and not the most interesting.

The hydro-therapeutic system will exert, and

is exerting now, we think, a positive influence in abating the nuisance of quackery in general. It will eventually put the community on their guard against the rash use of drugs, and be a standing warning to beware of those "matchless sanatives," "elixirs of life," "the great St. Peter's Oil," "High Phantom Bitters," "bi-chloride of gold," "salvation grease," "the spleen regulator," "golden hocus-pocus," etc., etc. It is stated by good authority that from forty-five to fifty millions in our country change hands every year in the traffic of patent nostrums, robbing the poor and the ignorant, and increasing the army of chronic sufferers at a fearful rate. The practice, too common in families, of dosing readily for every little complaint, even the most trivial, we may hope will soon be superseded. A convert to our new system, if afflicted with soreness of throat, for instance, is not obliged to rely upon drugs, which he may misuse, and which may effect a cure at the expense of his constitution. He has a harmless specific in the wet compress, in connection with gurgling, using cold water, which will kindly reduce the inflammation distressing him, and administer a quiet sleep. For all the other evils for which a judicious parent can safely prescribe without calling in a physician, he has a safer and surer remedy than can be found in the pharmacopœia.

We are not so sanguine as to expect that a large body of the people will at once, or very soon, be equally wise. The world moves slowly when it moves in the right direction. Our predictions have reference to a period remote enough not to disturb the equanimity of the present race of nostrum-venders and quack practitioners very much. Nevertheless, we trust, as Sir Bulwer Lytton, that a favored few, increasing in number and hastening the consummation, may verify our modest anticipations.

Why is it that evidence of a new idea travels slowly? It is on account of the intense influence habit has over man. We are also naturally conservative; we love to adhere to the methods of our fathers and grandfathers. We are naturally lazy; the majority of us prefer to have others do our thinking. Voltaire once said that every new truth experiences a treatment that ambassadors of civilized nations at the court of savages have to endure and go through with; it is after many obstacles, affronts, and insults that they receive a final hearing.

Pythogoras, having finished his new doctrine with reference to the multiplication table, as a sacrifice to the gods slaughtered one hundred steers; and now, ever since, when a new truth is proclaimed, the bovine tribe sends up an awful roar. They, the bovines, have also seriously shaken their heads because Prisznitz was but a peasant, a plain farmer. We say that the men of marked genius, the most noted reformers and benefactors of the human race, were ever men of low birth and modest education. The grandest religious reformer was the son of a carpenter's wife. His name was Jesus.

The greatest poet the world ever produced was a wool dealer (at one time a poacher), and an actor, who never sat within the walls of a high school or a college. His name was William Shakespeare.

One of our favorite philosophers, the man whom Napoleon credited with having exercised the most powerful influence in the development of rational education, at the beginning of the nineteenth century was a runaway apprentice of a watchmaker, and had never visited a university. His name was Rousseau.

The man who discovered the true art of healing disease was a peasant—Vinzenz Prisznitz.

It is a remarkable fact, also, that he first experimented on his horses. The German farmer is known to be proud of good stock. It is at the same time known that horses, next to men, have been the greatest sufferers from drug-medication. Tenderness, produced by it and other effeminating influences, have caused degeneration. The sickliness and nervousness of our present horse is observed everywhere, and much regretted. Why the handsomest and most useful should be the sickliest, has never been much investigated by the most intelligent of animals. Just in proportion as they are subjected to bloodletting, blistering, and poisoning by drugs, are they sickly or robust. The English racer is almost as rheumatic and hysterical as a first-class society woman; the farmer's horse shows more sense and better health; the Canadian pony is of hardy blood and of more steady service; but the horse of the red man never knows sickness, nor does his rider. Herein lies the strong moral of Prisznitz's system.

> "Out of the shadows of night
> The world rolls into light;
> It is daybreak everywhere."
> —LONGFELLOW.

Speaking of the great obstacles and popular opposition new ideas have most generally to contend with, we cannot close this subject without noting on the other hand the honesty and courage of a few prominent men, who, by their own conscience, were compelled to leave their old associates and to step out boldly for new light. Wo quote here a few lines from Dr. Pereira, one of the most celebrated standard medical writers.

Referring to the danger of using drug medicines *ad libitum*, he says: "Several noted physicians, aa Murray and Thompson, consider opium as primarily stimulant; some others, as Cullen and Barbier, regard it as sedative, which is just the contrary of stimulant. Dr. Meyer considers it as a stimulant to the nerves and a sedative to the muscles and digestive organs. Orfila regards it as neither, while others, as Mueller, call it an alterative." Here are five standard writers and physicians considering one of our most common yet powerful drugs in five different and contradictory ways, and, of course, must give it for exactly opposing objects.

Dr. Pereira also speaks thus of mercury: "By several writers, as Cullen, Young, and Eberle, it is put in the class of sialogogues; by Thompson, Edwards, and others, among the excitants; by Conradi and Horn it is called a sedative, and by Dr. Philips it is said to be stimulant in small doses and sedative in large ones. By Murray it is placed among tonics; by another, Vogt, among the *resolrentia;* by Sunderlin, among the liquefacients; by the followers of Brousais it is put in the line of revulsives; by the Italians, as contra-stimulants; but by Barbier it is placed among the '*incertæ sedis,*' or those drugs whose nature is not understood."

After reading the above, one is hardly surprised to find that another medical writer "once upon a time" exclaimed that the word *physician* should be defined as "a man who puts drugs, of which he knows nothing, into the human stomach, of which he knows less."

Of the celebrated Dr. Radcliffe much has been written, but much remains to be said. He was probably the most eccentric and at the same time the most successful physician of his day. Although he practiced medicine for many years, he had as great a contempt for physic as he had for physicians as a class, avowing it as his opinion that the whole art might be written on one sheet of paper. It may be doubted whether a more luminous lesson was ever given to the sick than his declaration that, when a young man, he possessed twenty remedies for every disease, but before the end of his career as an active practitioner, he found twenty diseases for which he had not one reliable remedy.

And how much is this in opposition to, or how interesting in comparison with, our old-time country doctor of not so very long ago, sitting by the bedside with a grave and serious countenance, his timepiece in one hand, the other gently pressing the pulse of his patient, who is looking up to him and anxiously watching the amount

of shaking the doctor's head may develop in
order to diagnosticate a bad case of ——? for
which the remedy, in his own mind, is probably
already fixed upon.

> Thus we, our hellish boluses compounding,
> Among these vales and hills surrounding,
> Worse than the pestilence have passed.
> Thousands were done to death from poison of my giving;
> And I must hear, by all the living,
> The shameless murderer praised at last.
>
> — FAUST.

Nine-tenths of the faith in drug medication
is maintained by the halo of antiquity. A certain
selection, or sets of remedies, mostly of the
"patent order," have their run in the same family
for many generations, and are often considered
indispensable, although their ultimate effects most
certainly are chronic derangements of the digestive organs in one form or another. Here is the
way Edward Eggleston[1] expresses the same idea:
"How many dogmas have lived for centuries, not
by their reasonableness (or logical propriety),
but by the impressiveness of trappings? Creeds
recited under lofty arches, liturgies chanted
by generations following generations, traditions
of law, however absurd, uttered by one big-
wigged judge, following a reverend line of ghostly
wigs gone before, that have said the same foolish
things for ages. These all take considerable

---

[1] Cf. "Faith Doctor," in *Century Magazine*.

advantage from the power of accessories to impose upon the human imagination. The divinity that hedges kings is the result of stage fixings, which make the little great, and half the horror inspired by the priest's curse is derived from the bell, the book, and some tall candles." He might have added that a very large number of doctors even of the present day live upon the credulity and ignorance of the people.

The *San Francisco Chronicle* published quite recently (September, 1891,) a historical sketch of pharmacy, covering a period between the fourteenth century and the middle of the eighteenth century, which has been largely quoted, and has found its way into some of our best papers over the Eastern States. Presenting dates and names of noted persons quite accurately, it must be accepted as having been compiled from good authority. We will be pardoned for placing before our readers a short extract therefrom:

"Included in the curious admixture of trades and occupations during the middle ages were those of the apothecary and the grocer, which, for several hundred years, were one and the same. Both sold certain articles used as medicines, or condiments, such as roots, herbs, ginger, pepper, cloves, cinnamon, anise, licorice, with gums, wax, and a few other things that were in daily use. It appears from this list that the pharmacopœia in those days was sufficiently simple. The trades of grocer and apothecary were regulated by the same edicts. In 1353, in France, it was ordered that no one should be allowed to carry on either kind of business, or to be employed in them, unless he were able to read the prescriptions, and as the ability to read was a rare accomplishment, it must have been difficult to find the necessary persons. Fraud was easy in the midst of universal ignorance. Herbs were sold that had lost their virtues, if they ever had them, or common garden-seeds were substituted. Spices came by long voyages from the Orient, and were often mixed with worthless substances. Finally, to avoid the frauds and errors arising from ignorance, it was found necessary to separate the trades of druggist and grocer, which, after numerous efforts, was finally accomplished in the early part of the sixteenth century.

"As the articles sold became more numerous, the adulterations became more common, and the frauds were naturally a source of frequent complaint. Among the substitutions was that of powdered horse bone for powdered stag bone, the latter being considered a sovereign remedy for diseases of the heart. The matter being investigated, it was discovered that many apothecaries never had any other herbs in their shops than common garden weeds, while one of the craft confessed on his deathbed that he had not had any real rhubarb in his shop for thirty years."

Then the *Chronicle* goes on through the fifteenth and sixteenth centuries, enumerating the therapeutics of those times: powdered skulls, of those executed for capital crimes; human fat (for rheumatism); the liver of the swallow burned, powdered, and mixed with wine to secure the fidelity of married women; the small bones of a rabbit's leg, for kidney trouble, etc., etc. We now resume with the seventeenth century:

"Van Helmont was a chemist, physiologist, and physician in Belgium, and one of the most celebrated men of his epoch. His learning did not prevent his sharing in the superstitions of his time. Among the remedies he recommended was a belt of live toads for dropsy, etc.

"Dr. Monnier was a French physician and sufficiently eminent to be the medical adviser of the Guise family. He believed in powdered bees and spiders as sovereign remedies; the skin of a rabid dog would cure hydrophobia, etc. A Dr. Charles enjoyed a great reputation that extended all over Europe. He was Professor of Chemistry at the Royal Gardens in France, member of the Academy of Sciences, etc. His titles to distinction are mentioned to throw into greater relief the extraordinary character of his pharmacopœia. Frogs, toads, centipedes, earthworms, ants, vipers, etc., were among his favorite remedies. His theories were endorsed by the writers of his time, notably by Mme. De Sevigne, who, in a letter to her daughter, attributes her excellent health to long indulgence in viper soup, not made of dried or powdered, but of live, reptiles; and she advises her correspondent 'to pray M. de Boissy to send her ten dozen live vipers from Poiton in cases, three or four in each, with moss and bran, that they may be perfectly comfortable.'

"Dr. Vallot, physician of Louis XIV., prescribed for his mother lozenges, of which pearls and gold were constituents. Among his most efficacious antidotes were certain kinds of clay, brought from the Isle of Lemnos, marked with Turkish characters and made of stony formations found in animals and fishes. Of the last, *Bezoar*[1] was the most famous. It was produced by a goat found in the far East, or counterfeited when

[1] In one of our modern medical lexicons, Bezoar is defined as a calculous concretion found in the stomach, intestines, and bladder of animals, and that formerly wonderful virtues were attributed to these Bezoars, five or six different kinds being available: that of the chamois or wild goat of Peru; of the antelope of India; Bezoar *Bovinum* (of the beef); Bezoar *Equinum* (of the horse), etc.

the genuine article could not be found, the real
and the counterfeit naturally having the same
curative power.   It was taken in the form of
powder, and its mode of operation, or its supposed
effect, were it now in use, would fall under the
head of *faith cure*."

The *Chronicle* winds up with the following
remarks of its own: "It appears from this brief
résumé of the subject, that the history of medicine
is the history of human credulity, at which we
can now well afford to laugh. But when a
hundred years hence, our descendants read the
newspapers that have come down to them from
us, the lists of nostrums, each with its record of
wonderful cures, and the advertisements of certain
quacks, *it is possible that we shall seem to them
scarcely less ridiculous*."

We have before us a small but remarkable
volume entitled, "The Physician Himself," a kind
of medical catechism, apparently written for
young men who have left the plow-handle or
the shoemaker's bench to become doctors; who
have been permitted to matriculate at one or
the other of our numberless colleges without a
classical, or even a normal education. If this
book or its circulation can be restricted or
confined to the eyes and the minds of those it
is intended for, it will at least do no harm; but

in the hands of the laity, it will add greatly to the distrust and skepticism of the average reader, and must naturally cause much laughter and ridicule. Dr. Cathell, its author, instructs these young men who have just entered the realms of Æsculapius without much preliminary schooling, but in possession of a "sheepskin," provided it is a "regular" one, that if they have not had the advantage of Latin, they should not fail to employ a good Latin scholar immediately to teach them at least enough to enable them to write their prescriptions with orthographic correctness. He states that "they can get one at a nominal cost," but that they should "advertise for him anonymously." He considers a little rudimentary Greek also quite useful; recommends a smattering of German, but omits to speak of Sanskrit.

He directs them how to place their "shingle," gives the size of its lettering, and advises them to put the "doctor" in front, instead of an M. D. behind their name. While it is strongly suggested never,—no, never, to consult with a homœopathist, an eclectic, or a hydro-therapeutist,—all these are put upon the level with "the old woman" who dabbles in medicine,—Dr. Cathell highly recommends homœopathic globules (unmedicated) for making "*placeboes*";[1] other-

---

[1] *Placeboes*—plural. "In medicine, a prescription more to please than to benefit a patient."—*Webster*.

wise he is ultra orthodox "regular," so much so—so very "regular," that he cautions his young doctors "to keep a straight face and to give minute directions concerning the manner and time of using these inert or innocent remedies, given simply to amuse people who are morbid on the subject of health, and you will do them double good."

"You will not only find that your *placebo* will amuse and satisfy people, but you will often be surprised to hear that some of them are chanting your praise and are willing to swear that they are cured of one or another awful thing by them. Cheated into a feeling of health by globules, or small doses of flavored water, or licorice powder, as if by a charm, some who seem to be magically benefited by a teaspoonful of nothing, will actually thank you for saving their lives."

Again: "Never send a patient to the drug store with a prescription for bread-pills. It is not right to make anyone pay for bogus medicine; besides, if from among all the articles in the pharmacopoeia you cannot devise some trifling *placebo* that is more plausible than bread-pills, you must have an unusual paucity of resources," etc

We quote now from another part,[1] Dr. Cathell instructing his young colleagues thus: "Quackery subsists almost entirely on credulity and ignorance; it is your duty to expose it in every shape; save as many from its evils as you can; wherever you meet it, lift its veil and show its unworthiness and the harm it does." Compare the essence or the nonsense of these last two sentences with each other and comment is unnecessary. But the most absurd part of the work is Dr. Cathell's revelation and the reason of the fact that well-cultured homœopathists in some localities often enjoy a lucrative practice: It is because people admire the sound of the first part of their title; they identify it with home, and they take their remedies because they consider them home-medicine, while *homœo* is derived from the Greek *homoios* (similar), and has no possible relation to hearth and home. He thinks they should style themselves "pathhomœists."

What a sad comment on the discerning power of the nineteenth century! Let us add, what a sad exhibition of short-sighted sophistry and selfishness promulgated and apparently protected under a "regular" certificate! We believe for one that the superstitious reverence for mere diplomas is fast passing away. If Dr. Cathell wishes to know why, we answer, it is because so many are held by men possessed of a spirit like his own, or by those he wishes to instruct by his "Physician Himself." It is but repeating a truism to say that it is the vice of all closely-organized bodies, that they are never up with the best of progress to the full light and knowledge of the times. It required five hundred years for Dr. Cathell's "regulars" to discover that a copious drink of pure fresh water, allowed to a patient in high fever, will not kill him; it took them one thousand years to find out that blood-letting nine times out of ten was next to a downright butchery.

The practice of scientific medicine is certainly a lofty calling, a very honorable profession, full of responsibility, and its honest and progressive disciples will ever be recognized and universally appreciated; but still, again, as Dr. Cutter states it, there are incompetent and dishonest men engaged in the practice of medicine, as well as in journalism, politics, and banking, or in the pulpit. If people would select their family physician with the same investigating care they employ in buying a horse or a sealskin sacque, never forgetting that the man makes the doctor, and would make their selection only after serious consideration, the profession would be more satisfactory to patient and physician.

"Was die Wissenschaften am meisten retardirt, ist: dass Diejenigen, die sich damit beschäftigen ungleiche Geister sind. Wer die Menschen betrügen will muss vor allen Dingen das Absurde plausibel machen. Es giebt Pedanten, die zugleich Schelme sind, und das sind die Allerschlimmsten."—*Gœthe.*

NATURAL LENGTH OF HUMAN LIFE.

When one of us poor creatures dies, we ask at once, Of what disease? and we ask it as though death by disease were a part of nature's proper course! Man should die of old age, without complaint, without pain. Nature wills it so, and so die all wild animals; so die, too, all men who have not quitted the protecting arms of nature and her laws. But among us, how many die at present of old age or without pain? Not one in a thousand.

Still more. It is nature's will that men should not only die without disease, but that they should live without pain. Man's natural condition and relations have been so perverted, however, that their true laws can now be hardly recognized. What is the natural duration of human life in a healthful climate? All analogies and strict comparison drawn from the animal world, referring to the period of growth in connection with the length of life, fix man's life at from one hundred and fifty to two hundred years! Reader, do you smile at this? Go among the Arabians, at least among those tribes whose only drink is water or

milk, and you will still find men two hundred
years old; you will find many who at one hundred are in full possession of their faculties.
Even in Europe, during the last three centuries,
individuals have lived to the age of two hundred,
and it may here be confidently affirmed that they
have not lived beyond a natural period, but that
most men die before attaining it.

In the register of St. Leonard's Church, in London, is an entry which one might feel disposed to
doubt, if it were not fully and officially attested.
It is as follows: "Thomas Carn, born 28th Jan.,
1588, died 1795. He lived to the age of 207, and
saw 12 British Sovereigns on the throne." [1]

A great number of notices (resting upon good
authority) of the length of human life in ancient
times have come down to us, from which it
appears that the average duration of life in
modern times is really much less than it was
among the nations of antiquity. Several centuries
of corruption preceded the age of Vespasian
(9 B. C.), yet in his time were counted, over
a small territory, thirty-four persons of one
hundred years and over, forty between one
hundred and ten and one hundred and forty, and
two over one hundred and fifty. [2]

[1] For a remarkable collection of longevity instances, see Graham's
"Science of Human Life."

[2] Von Mueller's "Universal History."

At present, seventy years is considered a long life. The most who suffer from chronic diseases die between fifty and seventy. And these fifty or seventy years—are they *Life?* It is mostly a long disease, a chronic death, which lasts from fifty to seventy years before it is completed. From the time when the doctors and nurses first drink success to the new comer, may be dated the beginning of that disease which we call life. But it makes no difference. When that death-rattle is heard, the friends console themselves with stating that they did all that lay in human power; they called in the doctor, or perhaps a whole conference of doctors, and—thus all is explained.

So we live, and so we die! And in what forms do we go through the last half of our lives? In such forms that the artist must betake himself to the Bedouins of Africa, or to the red man of the plains, for good models; we can only serve for caricatures. It is the order of nature that every creature shall retain that form, even to old age, which he or she looks at the period of most perfect development. This law holds good for animals and men; even for those domestic animals which are not destroyed by excess of labor. Can you, by his form, distinguish whether the horse or the hound stands before you in the ful-ness of his strength, or in his decline? No! You must open his mouth to ascertain it. The same law prevails among men in a state of nature. The woman retains to old age the shape of her twentieth year, and still more certainly the man. You cannot, from the form of an Indian warrior, determine whether he is in his twentieth or in his sixtieth year; you can only decide it by his countenance. For the face is in man the natural index of his age, as the teeth are to the horse, the antlers to the stag, the rattle to the snake, etc.

With us, at present, when by some chance a woman of forty or fifty has retained the figure of her younger days, every one wonders at the prodigy, forgetting that it should be thus with all. After thirty years they lose the full and well-proportioned form of youth, and there comes either the disease of obesity to hang weights about them, or leanness that makes them the symbols of starvation. A well-proportioned figure, full and firm, with elastic muscular action, is rare enough at any age, but almost unheard of in advanced life. Do you believe that nature meant that after thirty years man should be either a waddling cask or a stalking skeleton? Emphatically no! She never works in mockery or derision.

What, then, shall we do to regain manhood for ourselves or for our posterity? Go back to the woods and become wild again? No! We need give up none of the true comforts and enjoyments of civilization and "modern improvements"; we need only unite with them the advantages of savage life. Return to simple diet, be regular in our habits, use the "Indian clubs" and dumbbells, in place of the tomahawk, take our baths every day; in short, live out the doctrines heretofore presented.

SWIMMING, AS A PHYSICAL ACCOMPLISHMENT, AS A THERAPEUTICAL AGENCY, AND AN ORTHOPEDIC GYMNASTIC.

When the ancient Athenians wished to designate a man who was good for nothing, they were accustomed to say, "He cannot even swim," which shows how important the art was considered by them. With modern society it is by no means a common accomplishment, notwithstanding we are often placed in situations in which it may at any moment become of more importance to us than all the rest of our boasted acquirements put together, and even essential to the preservation of our lives, nay, other lives, dearer than our own. Really good swimmers, men who might cross the Hellespont with their strong limbs, as Leander did, for love, and Byron after him for glory, are very rare indeed among us.   Even our sailors are not infrequently unable to swim a single stroke.

As a hygienic agency and a means of physical culture, swimming very properly takes a high rank.   In fact, we consider it to be, within the range of its application, one of the most efficient of bodily exercises.   Its free and graceful movements give healthful action to all the important muscles; the contact with the animate waves, so full of magnetic virtue, which it involves, invigorates our body, and the conquest of a new element which it secures, dilates the whole being with a sense of triumph and of power.

Everybody should learn to swim—women no less than men. "Beauty, the mother of love," according to one of the myths of the ancients, "is the daughter of the waves and of light." Water and sunshine still acknowledge their relationship, and the fairest forms grow fairer still in the animate embrace of the limpid elements. The maidens of the Pacific Islands swim like nymphs; so do most of the Italian, the Mexican, and South American women, and many others. Our wives and daughters should follow their example in this matter; and we earnestly recommend our fair readers (as well as those not so fair) who have not already acquired these facilities, to commence their lessons at the earliest opportunity.

As a therapeutical agency for overcoming disorders of the digestive organs, torpor of liver, habitual constipation, etc., swimming cannot easily be overestimated. The salutary effects of a full bath in connection with the almost total, yet gentle, activity of the muscular system are readily observed, and with proper management of temperature and time may be enjoyed by many invalids laboring under the above derangements in a chronic form to great advantage and without the slightest degree of danger.

Swimming, as a treatment for deformities, or orthopedic gymastic.

Lateral obliquities of the spine, round-shoulderedness, and all other curvatures are the consequences of muscular debility, often either inherited of scrofulous parents, or brought on by bad habits. School discipline, regarding proper furniture and its use, or the attention of teachers to the positions of their pupils, has been much neglected; has never been fully recognized or administered. It should form a part of school hygiene, as its application would prove a great blessing. Careful observations have shown that at least one-half of our youths, boys as well as

7

girls, are affected with some degree of distortion of the spine.

Medical examinations recently made at the public schools of New York were brought to the conclusion that thirty-three per cent. of the girls and twenty-five per cent. of the boys in attendance in those institutions are affected with more or less spinal curvature.

The late Doctor Sir John Forbes, an eminent physician and well-known medical author of London, writes: "We recently visited in a large town a boarding-school containing forty-six girls, and we learned, on close and accurate examination, 'that there was not one of the girls who had been at the school two years that was not more or less crooked.'"

As a spine exercise, swimming is the safest and most efficient of gymnastics. The mere position under instruction brings into play and action all the muscles of the vertebræ, the strength and elasticity of which promote an erect and graceful carriage, and, if the exercise is continued through several seasons, will correct or greatly improve many spinal deformities.

In Europe, the different governments observe an extensive interest in physical culture of the people, and the German Empire takes the lead. Every university, every high school, and every regiment of its vast army, has its own swimming school. Every subaltern officer has to be a well-trained and qualified swimming-teacher, and every soldier during his first year of service learns to swim, not only in nudity, but in uniform, including full marching equipments and carrying his musket. All the horses of their cavalry are trained to cross large rivers, carrying their riders quietly, orderly, and under perfect discipline. The horse, as all quadruped animals, is a natural swimmer, but without this training there might often be confusion, caused by a few becoming fractious in the absence of experience.

In this country, it is only ten years since the cadets at West Point and at Annapolis first enjoyed the use and advantage of a systematic swimming school. Previous to that time, it may appear strange, even the young United States naval officer was sent to sea without the slightest reference to his capacity as a swimmer. These schools were built according to the plans and specifications of the author, who began to agitate the importance and necessity of them in the year 1871, under the then presidency of General Grant, who became at once much interested. But it was left to the patience and perseverance of General Howard and the late Admiral Porter to finally push an extra appropriation through Congress for this purpose. After two extended visits to Washington, and at the time we were building a *natatorium* in Baltimore (1881), we were one day pleasantly surprised by receiving a message from Admiral Porter, announcing that, if agreeable, Commander Greene, with the master mechanics of the Navy Yard, would call for observations and final instruction. The Annapolis school was built that year, West Point following suit two years thereafter. We cannot conclude, in justice to the memory of General George G. Meade, at that time (1871) our next-door neighbor in Philadelphia, without stating that he was first in urging our visit to Washington, furnishing valuable letters of introduction, and speaking in high terms of the enterprise and its necessity. Neither will it appear egotistical for the author here to state that he is justly considered the pioneer in this branch of physical education in this country, meaning in-door swimming schools in connection with gymnasia, having successfully introduced in the swimming department the Prussian military system of instruction.

The Philadelphia Natatorium and Physical Institute was originally built by a stock company, the organization of which was accomplished by the exertion of Mr. M. Hlasko, at the time a citizen of Philadelphia and a great reader and enthusiast of ancient history and ancient tales, speaking of Roman strength and beauty and of Grecian grace and loveliness. The institution was organized and incorporated with a board of directors, the late Dr. Paul B. Goddard elected its president, and Joseph W. Drexel, Esq., treasurer, and opened under our management in 1860. Others since have been built under our personal supervision in Chicago, Baltimore, and several smaller towns, and it is with pride we state that to-day over ten thousand girls and young women, former pupils and all good swimmers, and many more on the side of the male sex, can testify to the efficiency of the system and the great benefit received from its practice.

HORSEBACK RIDING AND ITS SANITARY IMPORTANCE.

Riding on horseback, when acquired and practiced under proper instruction, referring to correct position and management of the horse, is one of the most pleasant and health-restoring out-door exercises in the whole range of hygienic gymnastics. For expanding the lungs and energizing the digestive system, for dyspeptics and consumptives in the early stages of the disease, it is of the greatest advantage. In the South and far West it is a universal accomplishment, while in the Northern and Eastern States it is not as yet sufficiently appreciated.

Dr. John M. Keating, of Colorado Springs, in an article contributed to the *Medical Record*, says: "After one has lived for even a few months in the far West, the subject of horseback exercise becomes a topic most absorbing. The pure air and almost constant sunshine invite one to lead an out-door life. The shady mountain passes, with a constant change of superb views, from cañons to peaks, and the glimpses of the vast expanse of plains with a horizon like the ocean, tempt one to take exercise which otherwise he would probably not have strength or energy to do. Then to canter on the prairie is so fascinating that one scarcely knows when to stop. 'To sleep in a tent and live on one's horse by day,' is a prescription that has very frequently saved the life of an otherwise doomed mortal; but I am sorry to say that I fear that it has been greatly abused, and that rash exposure has been guilty of taking to an early grave many who otherwise would have grown well and strong.

"It should be remembered that riding, even walking one's horse, gives no little exercise; it is naturally fatiguing, indeed exhausting, and one should bear in mind an axiom in the treatment of pulmonary diseases—never to fatigue, but to exercise gradually as the strength increases.

"Time and again, doctors have told me that patients have come to them in various stages of consumption, some, indeed, in a very debilitated and dangerous condition, buoyed by hope and armed with instruction from the home doctor, 'to sleep in a tent and take plenty of horseback exercise.' Carrying out this advice a fatal hemorrhage would often prove its harmfulness.

"In the studies that I have made in various forms of physical exercise especially beneficial to children and delicate women, I have been impressed with the fact that the perfection of exercise was that which moderately brought into concerted action all the muscles of the body and tended to symmetrically develop the individual, and that well-sustained exercise of this character equalized the circulation, produced no congestions or strain, and stimulated arterial and venous flows. For a man, horseback riding possesses all these qualities; but, strange to say the woman is so hampered by fashion that I am more and more impressed with the fact that in a large number of cases riding with the side-saddle does far more harm than good."

Dr. Keating then explains and demonstrates the violation of physiological laws, as committed by the position of women in the saddle, as at present in vogue, and continues: "However straight a woman may try to hold herself in the position she assumes on a horse, she will gradually fall into the habit of a slight lumbar curvature to the left, and it stands to reason that, for one who rides a great deal, a want of symmetry in development on both sides will be sooner or later noticeable. I believe this is obviated to a certain extent in England by the movable pommel, the young rider being obliged to ride on one side one day and on the other the next day.

"I am surprised that those who have seen much of the diseases of women have not taken a more positive stand in this matter. There is no reason whatever, except the arbitrary dictates of fashion, why a saddle could not be so constructed that a girl could ride with equal comfort and grace as can her brother; moreover, she would get far better control of her horse, and there would be very much less danger of ovarian and uterine prolapses, bladder disturbances, lateral spinal curvatures, etc. Those who have had courage enough to try this innovation, have assured me that the difference in comfort was remarkable.

"In order to secure the advantages of riding astride, a woman should, I think, have a saddle constructed somewhat different from that used by men. This saddle should combine healthfulness, safety, and comfort. Healthfulness would require an erect, symmetrical posture of the rider, freedom from angles that would interfere with perfect circulation and would prevent any strain or pressure on the pelvic organs. Safety would give a firm seat, sure control of the horse, and an easier mount than can now be accomplished. Comfort would come from freedom, from restriction, and an easy seat," etc.

Dr. Keating closes with a minute description of a saddle, as he would recommend, which we omit.

Dr. Edwards, editor of the *Annals of Hygiene*, in last month's issue (February, 1892,) brings an interesting episode from the pen of the late Dr. Dio Lewis, which has a direct bearing upon the subject under discussion. He calls it a "Consumptive Romance," and it runs as follows:

"While practicing my profession in Buffalo, where I lived many years, the mail brought a note one evening requesting an interview with reference to the writer's health. He came next morning and said:

"'You see I am a young man; I came to America two years ago seeking my fortune. An old friend induced me to stop here, and now I am junior partner in the firm of G. T. & Co. My father, mother, and sister all died of consumption. I have been coughing and getting thin for about eight months. Please feel my pulse.'

"'What, ninety-five?'

"'That's about it, and in the evening I fancy it gets above one hundred.'

"'How about your breathing?'

"'Hills and stairs make me gasp. I have all the symptoms. I watched my sister, and know just how this terrible thing works.'

"'Night sweats?'

"'Not much; though occasionally my shoulders and neck are wet when I wake in the morning.'

"'Pain?'

"'I have several times had a severe pain under my shoulder-blade, and lately a dull aching just here under this collar-bone.'

"'Expectoration?'

"'I raise pretty freely in the morning.'

"'Prepare yourself, and let me listen.'   After listening at his chest awhile, I asked: 'Do you want me to tell you the truth, or humbug you with a nice story?'

"'The truth, doctor—the whole truth.'

"'Your lungs are in a bad way. The left lung, through all its upper part, is a mass of tubercles. Some of them have softened. The upper part of the right lung is slightly tubercular, but the softening has not yet begun.'

"'There can be no mistake?

"'I can mark the exact outline of the deposit.'

"With reddened eyes and trembling voice he said: 'I wouldn't mind it for myself, but a beautiful girl, whom I love better than my own life, expects me to come to her next winter. It will kill her, sir. Of course nothing can be done for me?'

"'Let me listen again very carefully, and then you must give me a day to think of it.'

"When he came next morning, I said: 'I have written a letter to your friend in England. Here it is. Read it, and hurry it off by the first mail.'

"'DEAR LADY:—Your friend, George C., has come to me about his health. I have examined his lungs and find that he has consumption. In the ordinary course of things he will die in about six months. He has told me with streaming eyes of the crushing grief this news will bring to you. My dear lady, if you will come to us, you and I will save him. I am your friend,' etc.

"The young man withdrew to a window, and when he could command his voice, said: 'Are you serious? I thought this disease was incurable as death.'

"The letter was sent. A horse and saddle were purchased. He was so impressed with the necessity of doing as I prescribed that he started on his morning ride, in all weathers, at exactly eight o'clock. He rode, as soon as the first soreness disappeared, three and a half hours every day. In a month it was three hours in the forenoon, and two in the afternoon. In a little more than two months Mary arrived, while George was out with his horse. She came at once to me, and with painful eagerness asked, after speaking her own name, 'How is George? For mercy's sake, don't tell me he is worse!'

"My wife insisted that the marriage should come off at our house. We all cried, and that does seem so absurd at a wedding!

"Of course parts of his lungs do not breathe, but he is a healthy man and does a large amount of work. His wife still writes to us. She closed her last letter with the words: *'May God bless you for saving the life of my noble husband!'*

"I believe that nothing but a saddle-horse could have saved him. Of course, I do not disparage other features of the needed regimen, but the saddle-horse is the *Hamlet* of this play. I do not believe in 'specifics,' but the saddle in consumption comes very near one. Dr. Holmes's saying, that 'the outside of a horse is good for the inside of a man,' is emphatically true in diseases of the lungs.

"The needed improvement in digestion and assimilation cannot be secured without much exercise, and lungs in those conditions forbid all exercise but the saddle. While a single flight of stairs or a slight hill will make the patient gasp, he can ride a hard trotter ten or twenty miles.

"The use of whisky and drugs in consumption proves the patient's ignorance and the doctor's necessity."

Having allowed considerable space to these two healthful exercises, swimming and horseback riding, we must not neglect to mention at least a few other pastimes which may equally be given a place among legitimate gymnastics, namely: Rowing, bicycling, skating, lawn - tennis, and croquet. All the above are valuable exercises, because they are appropriate for both sexes, because they invite to life in the open air, and combine amusement with health-promoting muscular activity.

The position on the bicycle, however, we are sorry to observe, is not always what it should be; many young riders assume a stooping attitude, apparently under the mistaken idea that such an ungraceful position increases the speed of their wheel. The spine should always be held perfectly erect, the eye striking the ground at least five yards ahead, and of course shoulders drawn back, with elbows close to the body.

PART III.

Hygiene—Health—Regimen—Health in its Fullness—The Science of Preserving It.

HYGIENE embraces a knowledge of health in man, both individually and in society, the rational management and methodical use of everything essential to life, as air, food, water, light, exercise, sleep, dress, etc. When properly modified, at times intensified, and judiciously managed, these essentials or vital agencies are perfectly capable of producing remedial effects in disease preferable to the whole pharmacopœia of the drug-shop. Nine-tenths of the diseases have their origin in functional derangements, the regulations or repair of which in proper time can be better accomplished by hygienic discipline, as indicated above, and good nursing, than by pills or powders. Mechanical injuries, dislocations, and displacements, organic lesions, etc., of course require the skill and management of the surgeon.

THE AIR WE BREATHE.

Air in its pure and natural state is an invisible, transparent, inodorous, and elastic fluid, surrounding our earth to the height of from forty-five to fifty miles. Its chemical constituents are twenty parts oxygen and eighty parts nitrogen. Oxygen is its vital part; nitrogen is required to dilute it. It also contains a small part of carbonic acid gas and has floating in it various aqueous vapors and other terrestrial emanations, which often vary, according to geographical and topographical conditions; hence a change of air may be found serviceable, and often very important. for the prevention and cure of morbid conditions. Its supply in abundance is essential to life in all its forms.

Persons or animals confined in close rooms, breathing and re-breathing the same air until its oxygen is exhausted, will certainly be relieved by death in a short time. A lamp or candle will expire when all the oxygen is consumed, it being as essential to combustion as to respiration. Physiologists have calculated that the amount of fresh air required for an ordinary man is from eight to ten cubic feet per minute. Two hundred persons shut up in a room sixty by thirty and thirty feet high, thus containing nearly sixty thousand cubic feet of space, would render that room and its air unfit for respiration in about five hours. Imperfect ventilation, therefore, in crowded rooms, in churches, in schools, factories, etc., especially in the evening when artificial light is employed (an ordinary-sized gas-burner consumes about as much oxygen as four adults), is a common source of debility and disease.

When Florence Nightingale returned from her arduous sojourn, at the close of the Crimean war, she delivered some very interesting lectures in England. Relating her experience in the hospitals and referring to the various reforms introduced by her, she spoke of the difficulties she encountered in having the rooms of the sick and wounded well ventilated by day and by night. She found frequent objections, even in the minds of the surgeons, to drawing fresh air at night. But she succeeded, after presenting some powerful arguments in favor of her demand, in having the apartments in a healthful condition, during the night as well as by day. "Why," she pleaded, trying to overcome a strong popular prejudice, "at night, all air is night air," and it is correct. While the absence of the sun reduces the amount of atmospheric electricity at nights, the air, freshly introduced, is still much purer than that which has been inhaled and exhaled many times in succession and hence vitiated with poisonous gases.

We often meet with the same mistaken ideas in private houses. The bedrooms are frequently badly located for thorough ventilation, and the case rendered worse by close windows, or at times by thick curtains and hangings with which the beds are so carefully surrounded as to prevent the possibility of the air being renewed. The consequence is that we are breathing vitiated air during the greater part of the night; that is, during more than a third part of our lives; and thus the period of repose, which is necessary for the renovation of our mental and bodily vigor, becomes a source of disease. Sleep under such circumstances is very often disturbed, and always much less refreshing than when enjoyed in a well-ventilated apartment. It often happens, indeed, that such repose, instead of being followed by renovated strength and activity, is succeeded by a degree of heaviness and languor which is not overcome till the person has spent some time in pure air. Nor is this the only evil arising from sleeping in ill-ventilated apartments. When it is known that the blood undergoes most important changes in its circulation through the lungs by means of the air which we breathe, and that these vital changes can only be effected by the respiration of pure air, it will be easily seen how the healthy functions of the lungs must be impeded by the inhaling, for many successive hours, of the defective air of such rooms, and how the health must certainly suffer, or be destroyed,

8

by respiring impure air as by living on unwholesome or innutritious food.

In cases of children or young persons predis-
posed to pulmonary debility, it is of still more
urgent consequence that they should breathe
fresh air by night as well as by day, securing
them a continuous renewal of air in their nurs-
eries, bed-rooms, etc. Let a mother, who has
been made anxious by the sickly looks of her
children, go from pure air into their bed-rooms
in the morning before a window has been raised
and mark the state of atmosphere—the close,
oppressive, and often fetid, odor of the room;
and she may cease to wonder at their pale, sickly
appearance. Let her pay a similar visit some
morning, after means have been taken to secure
sufficient ventilation— a full supply and continual
renewal of the air in their bedrooms during the
night, and she will be able to account for the
more healthy looks of her dear ones, which is
sure to be the consequence of supplying them
with proper air to breathe.

In September, 1862, a few days after the battle
of Antietam, the author was summoned by wire
to Burkittsville, a small village in Maryland,
where a brother, serving in the Union army, lay
wounded in one of the field hospitals. It was
rather late in the evening when we reached the

place and had located the patient, yet by courtesy
of the surgeon in charge we were invited to
enter the hospital at once, where brother and
about one hundred and sixty others had found
accommodations. It was a small brick church
ninety by forty, with one floor and a gallery on
three sides. The occupants were of both armies,
representing the blue and the gray, and all had
gone through an amputation of some kind;
brother we found minus his left leg. It was
after eleven o'clock and the majority of the patients had gone to sleep, many of them, as we
supposed, by the aid of some sedative. There
was not a particle of an opening for a little fresh
air to steal in; the atmosphere was heavy with
poison, fearfully fetid, the whole place a veritable
"hole of Calcutta." When the kind surgeon
noticed our agony in attempting to breathe, he
explained that he had to yield to a large number
of requests to keep the windows closed on account
of insufficient bed-clothes. The men were lying
on straw and some of them had only their coats
or blouses to cover with, but he observed
that the Southerners in a body objected to the
night air always. Next morning we rented two
pleasant rooms at the parsonage and succeeded
in making poor brother very comfortable. We
then assisted during several evenings thereafter

to convert the Confederates at the hospital. After they were furnished with blankets, they were much pleased to have every window open, or as many as was necessary, according to the state of the thermometer, although some informed us that they never before slept in a room with windows open at nights when at home.

These views, of course, have no bearing on localities entirely unfit for human habitation. The swamp lands and districts where stagnant water collects and proper drainage is impossible, where poisonous evaporation goes on by day and by night, should be shunned as pestilence itself.

THE CLOTHES WE WEAR.

Healthful dressing is a subject to which, generally, very little attention is paid, though it is a matter of great importance to all, and especially to those whose circulation has been more or less effected and disturbed by chronic sickness. We should wear nothing next to the skin the substance of which is not a good heat conductor. Bodily comfort depends largely upon a proper circulation and upon a healthful action of the skin and stomach. We generate animal heat just in proportion to its waste. If we, in severe weather, for instance, wrap up our anatomy in several sets of underwear, we will feel probably very comfortable for a few days at least; but after a certain time, and by degrees, such extravagant protection will lose its charm, and will not only not protect any more, but will have the very opposite tendency. Our skin becomes less and less active, the capillary circulation towards the periphery of the body gradually becomes sluggish, the desire for food is diminished—in short, nature will accommodate itself to this superabundance of wrappings, and leave us in the cold, or oblige us to call for still more underclothes again. Wool is a very poor conductor of heat; cotton comes very near to it; silk is worse, and will even neutralize electricity. The great process of change of matter, as we have demonstrated before, is the essence and motive-power of life. Waste matter is constantly thrown out by the action of the skin, and this can only be done by the animal heat always active within. It is a well-known fact that heat is expansive, but this expansion is interfered with if the substances worn next to the skin are bad heat-conductors.

Too warm dressing, therefore, is considered as impairing the digestive organs. This is the reason why the habit of wearing wool or even cotton next to the skin is objectionable. Silk has a still more debilitating effect. The ancients were acquainted with this fact, for we read in Herodotus and Xenophon that the Medes were despised by other nations for being known to wear silk next to the skin. On the same ground they considered the linen of Egypt the most healthy under-dress. It is a better conductor of heat than any of the above mentioned substances. The more our skin is kept in direct contact with the atmosphere surrounding us, in other words, the more we provide for a free exhalation from our whole body, the more easily we retain a comfortable degree of heat, even in cold weather; but the increase of protection in severe changes or low temperatures should consist of heavier material in our outer garments, not in additional underwear, which cannot be removed on entering heated rooms. Bodily comfort is more or less a matter of habit, and we must discriminate between the natural sensations of health and the morbid sensitiveness produced by false customs. Some persons may wrap their bodies in flannel under-garments and at times duplicate them, yet will indulge in a shivering paroxysm at every breath of cold air, while others, more rational in their dress, endure the coldest weather with less discomfort.

Furs are worn in this country more for ornament than use. They are the warmest clothing

materials known, and by overheating the parts
of the body to which they are applied, render
them extremely susceptible to cold. The late
fashion of wearing sealskins in this, our moderate
climate, has increased the revenue of many
physicians. Custom has dealt more cruelly with
infants than with adults in the style of clothing.
Swathing, bandaging from head to foot with the
view of shaping the body; bandaging the abdomen to prevent the child from becoming "pot-
bellied," are fashions happily going into disrepute
under the reformatory teachings of hydro-therapeutic and physiological writers. The newborn
infant wants no bracing or artificial supporting
from the clothes, but perfect freedom and loose
garments sufficient to preserve the requisite
temperature.

Liebig says: "The mutual action between the
elements of the food and the oxygen conveyed by
the circulation of the blood to any part of the
body, is the fundamental source of animal heat.
In the animal body the food is the fuel; with
a proper supply of oxygen we obtain the heat
given during its oxidation or combustion. In
winter, when we take exercise in the cold atmosphere, and when, consequently, the amount of
inspired oxygen increases, the desire and necessity
for food containing carbon and hydrogen increases

in the same ratio; and by gratifying the appetite thus excited, we obtain the most efficient protection against the most piercing cold. A starving man is soon frozen to death; and every one knows that the animals of prey in the arctic regions far exceed in voracity those of the torrid zone."

Our clothing, then, is merely an equivalent for a certain amount of food. The more warmly we are clad the less urgent becomes the appetite for food, because the loss of heat by cooling, and, consequently, the amount of heat to be supplied by the food is diminished. Hence, it is natural that overclad people have a poor appetite, and are generally afraid of the slightest bit of cold air.

We will close this chapter with an incident, referring to the popular ignorance about heavy underwear and its injurious influence upon the circulation and nutrition. There came, at the beginning of October, to the Glen Haven Institute, during our connection with the faculty of that place, a man with more than ordinary intelligence, to be treated for chronic bilious diarrhœa and intermittent fever. By profession a mining engineer, he had been exposed to rough climate and bad diet in one of our Western territories, where the laws of health and life receive a very limited consideration. On examining his case, we found him inclosed in three sets of heavy red flannel underwear, his body much emaciated, his appetite very low, his skin yellow, death-like, smooth, glossy, but in its texture tough as leather; the pores of it tightly closed, and, of course, extremely sensitive against all contact with the air, even in a heated room and with the thermometer at seventy-five degrees. After a few weeks' treatment, with baths quite tepid at first, followed by strong frictions, the life and action of the skin had been sufficiently revived to make it appear advisable to reduce his stock of red flannel. These directions were met with serious opposition, the man almost crying like a child and saying it would give him his "death of cold," but gradually yielding to our better knowledge and experience, after two months' stay he had dispensed with all his flannel, and, his appetite improving, felt very comfortable, protected by one suit of "lisle-thread" underwear. He recovered his health completely in three months and two weeks.

The artificial habit of lessening the breathing capacity by means of stays, corsets, and tight dresses of the gentler sex, is now happily passing away, although these wasp-like waists which have deformed the female form for so many years, still *adorn* the fashion-plates of the magazines. Could the women of America fully appreciate the importance of dress as connected with respiration, and the relation of this function to their own health and happiness and the welfare of their offspring, the monthly importation of "Parisian cuts," turns, twists, fits, and misfits, would soon be replaced by reform dresses, loose as well as short, or something in the line of clothing that would still more emancipate the lungs from oppression most strange and entirely unnatural. Another common nuisance which females thoughtlessly inflict upon themselves is tight garters, which seriously interrupt the circulation, causing cold feet in winter, and develop varicose veins in the lower extremities.

THE FOOD WE EAT.

The present century has been fruitful of arguments, of anatomical, physiological, philosophical, and chemical controversy, concerning the question whether a man shall be considered a carnivorous or a herbivorous animal; or, whether a compromise is admissible, on the strength of which we accept him to be "half and half." On one side, as Bible authority, it is asserted that the Lord wanted us to be vegetarians: "And God said, Behold, I have given you every herb bearing seed which is upon the face of all the earth, and every tree, in which is the fruit of a tree yielding seed; to you it shall be for meat."[1] And here comes the other side, demonstrating that after the great flood the Lord spoke thus: "And the fear of you and the dread of you shall be upon every beast of the earth, and upon every fowl of the air, upon all that moveth upon the earth, and upon all the fishes of the sea; into your hand are they delivered. Every moving thing that liveth shall be meat for you," etc. The best writers on physiology are in the same quandary, one side demonstrating that by the shape of the human jaw, and the formation of the teeth, it is clear that we are not to be classified with the lion or the panther. On the other side, it is finally proven that our masticating apparatus is built for a mixed diet; that it has the same facility to dispose of and prepare for proper digestion meat as well as fruit and vegetables.

Cuvier remarks: "The natural food of man, therefore, judging from his structure, appears to consist of fruits, roots, and other succulent parts of vegetables," etc.

Dr. Dickson, the author of "Chrono Thermalism," observes: "The most cursory examination of the human teeth, stripped of every other consideration, should convince anybody with the

[1] Genesis 1.

least pretensions of brains, that the food of man was never intended to be restricted to vegetables exclusively."

Thomas Bell, surgeon dentist to Guy's Hospital, London, declares that "every fact connected with the human organization goes to prove that man was originally formed a frugivorous animal."

Dr. Carpenter,[1] alluding to the same dispute, declares. "Now, the condition of man may be regarded as intermediate between these two extremes. The construction of his digestive apparatus, as well as his instinctive propensities, point to a mixed diet as that which is best suited to his wants."

Of the ancients, Diodorus Siculus, Ovid, and Eatianus testify that the primitive inhabitants of the earth subsisted on a vegetable diet, while Pliny, Plutarch, and Porphyry speak favorably of the effects such diet has in developing bodily vigor, and enabling men to bear hunger, thirst, heat, or cold.

John William Draper, standard author on physiology, asserts that "universal experience, as well as direct experiment, proves that in the case of man, health cannot be maintained on a uniform diet, however it may be with animals. A mixed food, which varies from time to time, seems to be essential," etc.

[1] "Principles of Human Physiology.'

John C. Dalton, another well-known author, is even more positive in his views, expressing them in these words: "In the human subject, therefore, the teeth are evidently adapted for a diet consisting of both animal and vegetable food. Mastication is here as perfect as it is in the herbivora, though less prolonged and laborious; for the vegetable substances used by man, as already remarked, are previously separated to a great extent from their impurities, and softened by cooking; so that they do not require for their mastication so extensive and powerful a triturating apparatus."

Finally, animal substances are even more completely masticated in the carnivora, and their digestion is accordingly completed with greater rapidity.

Austin Flint, Jr., whose "Text-Book of Human Physiology" has been popular for many years, tells us that "we should live upon vegetable principles, taking them in part directly, and in part after they have been *prepared by animals*. As a rule, the nutritive principles in vegetables are relatively less abundant than in animal food, and the indigestible residue is, therefore, greater; but man and even carnivorous animals, *may be* nourished for an indefinite period by appropriate articles derived from the vegetable kingdom."

We will now close these consultations by quoting one more authority. L. Landois—"Third American and translated from the sixth German edition" (1889), by far the most comprehensive and the most scientific Human Physiology published during the nineteenth century. It says: "As far as his organization is concerned, man belongs to the omnivorous animals—that is, those that can live upon a mixed diet," etc.;[1] and again: "A man who tries to nourish himself on beef alone commits as great a mistake as the one who would feed himself on potatoes alone. Experience has taught people that man may live upon milk and eggs, but that in addition to flesh we must eat bread, potatoes," etc.[2]

Here, then, we have men of more than ordinary power, experience, and authority divided, and presenting a variety of theories on a simple food question which has troubled the minds of so many people, but especially those who are suffering the consequences of dietary transgressions, or who have been misinformed regarding their individual requirements.

Frederick the Great, when harassed once about the religion of the people in his domain, paid very little attention to some proffered advice, but remarked that in his empire every one should be

---

[1] P. 403.

[2] P. 405.

blessed and enter the kingdom of heaven strictly according to his own fashion, form, and desire.

Many great minds have left, as relics and memorials of their wanderings on earth, certain truth sand original thoughts, the close observance and sequel of which would often free and relieve science of much confusion, if people only would study and apply logically their teachings and their meaning. One of the greatest and most divine prognostications is given us by Humboldt in his physical geography: "In nature, as in life, we have *no genera, no species*, but only individuals." This short thesis is full of importance and rich in its bearing regarding the human family. It overthrows much of our ideas of classification, as applied to the races, the nationalities, to temperaments, to diseases, etc. In sickness we cannot treat two cases alike; we have just as many types of diseases to deal with as we have faces. We say, then, with Frederick, let every one live, be happy, and die in his own fashion. Let every one understand the elementary principles of physiology sufficiently to apply them to his daily diet. The human instinct, in healthy persons at least, is never misleading; in sickness, the physician will assist in discriminating, but let the patient's desire be heard always. Meat, well prepared and properly cooked for the

invalid's table, is easier of digestion than many vegetables. Venison, young mutton, or choice beef
is an excellent article of diet in many chronic cases.
Yet again, the complete abstinence from meat in
certain diseases might be of great advantage.

In this matter, as in all affairs of human concern,
the sum total of our practical wisdom consists in
obeying the laws of nature (instinct), and the sum
total of science should be the investigation and
discovery of the reasons why all laws of life
should and must be in harmonious operation
with the never-erring, never-changing dogmas of
nature.

The best animal food is, as has been indicated
before, that derived from the herbivora—beef,
venison, mutton, etc. Those animals which receive their nourishment directly from the vegetable kingdom, will most certainly afford a purer
and more wholesome meat than others who sub-
sist on other animals—the carnivora. Omnivorous animals, the bear, the swine, etc., that eat
indiscriminately vegetables or other animals, are
inferior to the purely herbivorous as food for
human beings. Of the hog, which eats everything,
whose filthy carcass is converted into a mass of
disease by the ordinary fattening process, we only
express our abhorrence. Although his flesh and
grease, under the name of pork and lard, are

staple and, strange to say, favorite articles of food throughout Christendom, common observation has long since traced the prevalence of scrofula, erysipelas, and a variety of glandular and eruptive diseases, *resulting from impure blood*, to their general employment. If there are any animals which should be exterminated from earth, mad-dogs and fattened hogs are among them.

If our worthy representatives at the courts of Berlin and Vienna, Hon. Phelps and Col. Grant, who have just succeeded in reopening the markets there for American pork and lard, were only in the position to negotiate and sign contracts with parties high in authority, and otherwise responsible, to take our entire crop for all time to come, what a blessing it would be for this country, although our sincere sympathy would go out largely to our cousins on the other side of the Atlantic. A quarter of a century would wonderfully improve, almost revolutionize, the health-condition of this nation; three-fifths of our physicians would be without occupation, and obliged to change their profession or emigrate.

It has been stated by writers on dietetics of reputed authority, that chronic diseases, skin eruptions, malignant ulcers, etc., which had resisted all remedial agencies under a mixed diet, were promptly healed under a vegetable regimen.

9

Dr. Lambe succeeded in cases of cancer, scrofula, pulmonary and other maladies, which had progressed to the incurable stage, in arresting their ravages and protracting the period of life for many years, after changing the diet of these patients to a strict vegetable discipline. The celebrated Dr. Twichell, of New England, once cured himself of a malignant tumor of the eye, which had troubled him for ten years, and which had been excised and cauterized, with but temporary benefit, by simply restricting himself to a diet of bread and cream.

These facts seem to strengthen the popular belief that the substances of the human body are pretty much made up by what we eat. If a man subsists on pork long enough, he will become pork. Look at the Laplanders, the Kamtschadales, the Esquimaux; the natives of New Holland and Van Diemen's Land, the Calmuck-Tartars, etc. Their principal food is fish, flesh, animal fats, and oils, and their intellectual and moral standard as inferior and depraved as their bodily organization.

Sailors, miners, soldiers in the field, and others whose mode of living had to be simplified by circumstances before the industry of canning and preserving came into vogue, or before it had been brought to such a general perfection as to embrace every article of diet, used salt pork as their principal diet. It was popularly considered exceedingly nutritious because its presence could be felt for a long time, while in truth the very principle applied at its packing, in order to keep it from putrefaction, makes it obnoxious and its digestion laborious, slow, and difficult. On sailing-vessels, we believe, it is still the staple food, very little change or reform of diet being observed. According to Dr. Beaumont's tables, its chymification requires from five to six hours, while that of venison is set down for one hour and thirty minutes.

Hares fed upon cabbage exclusively, acquire a disagreeable taste, resembling cabbage. Wormwood holds the same relation to the organization of the sheep; it is even less assimilable. Tobacco, salted meats, and alcoholic drinks, give to the human flesh a sharp, and to cannibals, a disagreeable taste. The cannibals of the Pacific isles have often affirmed that the flesh of the white men is less pleasing than that of the black. This is certainly not from any peculiarity of the white race, but because the sailors they have been in the habit of eating live on salt provisions, and are accustomed to indulge in tobacco and bad whisky or rum.

"That part of digestion which takes place in

the stomach has always been regarded as nearly, if not quite, the most important part of the whole process. The first observers who made any approximation to a correct idea of gastric digestion were Reaumur and Spallanzani, who showed by various methods that the reduction and liquefaction of the food in the stomach could not be owing to mere contact with the gastric mucous membrane, or to compression by the muscular walls of the organ; but that it must be attributed to a digestive fluid secreted by the mucous membrane, which penetrates the food and reduces it to a fluid form. They regarded this process as a simple chemical solution, and considered the gastric juice as a universal solvent for all alimentary substances. They succeeded even in obtaining some of this gastric juice, mingled, probably, with many impurities, by causing the animals upon which they experimented to swallow sponges attached to the ends of cords, by which they were afterwards withdrawn, the fluids which they had absorbed being then expressed and examined.

"The first decisive experiments on this point, however, were those performed by Dr. Beaumont, United States Army, on the person of Alexis St. Martin, a Canadian boatman, who had a permanent gastric fistula, the result of an accidental gunshot wound. The musket, which was loaded with buckshot at the time of the accident, was discharged at the distance of a few feet from St. Martin's body, in such manner as to tear away the integument at the lower part of the left chest, open the pleural cavity, and penetrate, through the lateral portion of the diaphragm, into the great pouch of the stomach. After the integument and the pleural and peritoneal surfaces had united and cicatrized, there remained a permanent opening of about four-fifths of an inch in diameter, leading into the left extremity of the stomach, which was usually closed by a circular valve of protruding mucous membrane. The valve could be readily depressed at any time, so as to open the fistula and allow the contents of the stomach to be extracted for examination.

"Dr. Beaumont experimented upon this person at various intervals from the year 1825 to 1832. He established during the course of his examinations the following important facts: First, that the active agent in digestion is an acid fluid, secreted by the walls of the stomach; secondly, that this fluid is poured out by the glandular walls of the organ only during digestion, and under the stimulus of the food; and, finally, that it will exert its solvent action upon the food outside the body as well as in the stomach, if kept in glass phials upon a sand bath at the temperature of one hundred degrees Fahrenheit. He made, also, a variety of other interesting investigations as to the effect of various kinds of stimulus on the secretion of the stomach, the rapidity with which the process of digestion takes place, the *comparative digestibility of various kinds of food*," etc.[1]

We will give the table of Dr. Beaumont's observations in a supplementary chapter, with other statistics.

FOOD RESOURCES — PRESENT AND FUTURE.

Philosophers and scientific writers on political economy and vital statistics have not yet been able to agree upon any satisfactory theory as to the proper size of population, and as to the present and future capability of this earth for satisfactory subsistence. Mr. Malthus has contended that population has a tendency to increase faster than the means of support and maintenance, unless some extraordinary counteracting causes be interposed. On this assumption, "war, pestilence, and famine" should be considered an especial piece of good fortune to keep the race down to the level of the means of subsistence. This, however, places our Creator in an attitude

---

[1] Dalton's " Physiology."

from which reason revolts. Mr. Doubleday, on the other hand, meets the position of Mr. Malthus with an opposite theory. He has undertaken to show that poverty is the principal cause of a rapid increase, and that a good degree of all modern comforts of life "deadens the principle of increase." He sustains the first clause of his proposition by adverting to the fact that the poor folks have, as a rule, the most children, and the latter part by quoting the well-known historical data that wealthy and luxurious families have generally but few children, and frequently run out, as have done wealthy and luxurious nations. Both these doctrines are too narrow, wicked, and superficial.

Great wealth and extreme poverty may be equally in violation of the natural condition of man; but this great earth has been wisely fashioned and made capable of yielding sustenance for all the beings created thereon, and for those who may follow in future generations hereafter. If men and nations are at variance with themselves, and make war upon each other; if some have usurped too much of our common domain, and others have not where to lay their heads; if men have deranged their social relations, perverted the laws of their own organization, and entailed upon themselves and society innumerable so-called *"permitted evils,"* let us pause long enough before we charge all these results to natural tendencies or special providences.

The actual productiveness of our earth is almost incredible to those who have never informed themselves or examined the subject closely. It is stated by good authority that under the best modern systems of agriculture and proper dietetics, Ireland, where now eight millions of human beings starve, or at times come very near to it, could healthfully sustain one hundred millions, and the soil of the United States is capable of producing more than food enough for all the inhabitants at present existing on this globe.

DRINKS, NATURAL AND ARTIFICIAL.

There is not the slightest doubt that water alone is the natural drink of man. All concoctions, as coffee and tea, malt or spirituous liquors, fermented juices of the grape, or of fruits of any kind, are the inventions of a false industry, and injurious to health. Although it is stated even by medical men that their moderate use may often be of good service, it is easy to prove that their salutary virtues are merely temporary, and may be compared in their action with nine-tenths of all popular drugs. Their benefit or tonic effects are of the same doubtful value as the whip appears to be when applied to a tired horse;

they exhilarate for a moment, produce apparently a slight increase of strength, or vital ambition, but the reaction therefrom is at the expense of exhausted and abused nature. The whip never gives a tired-out horse new strength.

We also see it often stated that men or women have lived to a good old age while they had indulged in the daily use of tea or coffee, or had drank their beer or their wine with regularity, yet who could tell, or contradict, how many years they might have added to their lives on earth had their habits been more in conformity with the laws of health? and how easily can we point out on the other side hundreds of cases where, by these indulgences not well controlled, the usefulness of persons has been cut short by premature death.

Water, if we consider its bearing on the chemical machinery of the universe, is, next to air, the most important element for sustaining life in all its variety. It forms the bulk of all organic bodies. The earth itself on its surface is covered by it to the extent of two-thirds, in fact nearly three-quarters, while probably four-fifths of it constitute its total organism. So is water an integral part of the human body, and the presence of an exact quantity thereof necessary for all vital functions. For instance:

In 100 parts of blood we have..............81 parts of water.
In 100 parts of lymph we have.............95 parts of water.
In 100 parts of saliva we have..............99 parts of water.
In 100 parts of bile we have...."'".........90 parts of water.
In 100 parts of woman's milk we have.....93 parts of water.
In 100 parts of brain we have..............80 parts of water.
In 100 parts of muscles we have...........77 parts of water.
In 100 parts of nerves we have.............70 parts of water.
In 100 parts of skin we have...............57 parts of water.
In 100 parts of tendons we have...........51 parts of water.
In 100 parts of bones we have..............46 parts of water, etc.

Or, within the whole organism an average of eighty per cent. of its total weight; hence, a man of one hundred and forty pounds represents, in substance, one hundred and twelve pounds of water, twenty pounds of which are constantly circulating through his system, mixed with his blood.

Thus, if we reflect upon the daily absorption and secretion of fluid-matter in a healthy body, we find that, under moderate temperatures, we part with about three and one-half pounds of water in the urine, with four and one-half to five pounds through the action of the skin, and with three-fourths to one pound by evaporation in the action of the lungs, or from eight to nine and one-half pounds total every twenty-four hours, which we return to the outer world, and which, of course, have to be replaced in order to retain the normal activity of our animal economy.

It appears plausible, then, that the purer and the fresher, the more natural and the more normal, our daily drinks may be, the easier will be their absorption and assimilation, and the less a tax they must be on the chemical performance of the human laboratory. In other words, if these fluids are replaced by pure spring water, it must naturally be more agreeable to an unsophisticated palate and more wholesome and beneficial to an honest stomach, than the same supply by coffee or tea, by alcoholic or other poisonous compounds, the so-called tonic, stimulating, or narcotic effects of which are, as we have stated, only temporary and of short duration, and the reaction therefrom being disagreeable and demoralizing in its effects on body and soul.

> " Though I look old,
>   I am strong and lusty;
>   For in my youth I never did apply
>   Hot and rebellious liquors to my blood."
>   SHAKESPEARE.

For thousands of years water has been considered a simple unit, and as such, was ranked with fire, air, and earth, as one of the four fundamental elements of our globe. It is only since 1781 that Cavendish and Lavoisier were successful in defining it as a compound. 100 parts of water (in weight) contain 11.1 parts of hydrogen and 88.1 parts of oxygen. In its pure state it is without color, without taste, and inodorous. It serves man in three different forms. As a fluid, it is useful in a great many ways too numerous to refer to in this space. At a temperature of 32° F., it changes its density and becomes ice, and at 212° F., it is steam. Its expansion in the latter process is remarkable, one cubic inch of water representing one cubic foot of steam; hence, water has 1728 times the weight of steam; the latter possessing five times the heat of boiling water.

The best drinking-water is found in the springs from the rocks (not limestone), or from a sandy subsoil among the mountains and in the forests, away from the densely settled tracts of mankind, where the deer comes for his nectar and the trout goes through his antics, jumping over the shells and stony pathway, up and up the crystal rivulet. But, alas! how few of us mortals can visit these fountains of nature's holy peace and purity and there imbibe her life-giving and soul-stirring liquid bliss with any regularity?

Next to spring water, rain water might be considered the purest of natural waters. Air is a constant constituent of, or admixture with, rain water. It contains also a slight trace of ammonia, which is probably a product of animal decomposition, and the cause of its readily running into putrefaction process.

Snow water does not differ materially from rain water, except in not containing air. That it is injurious to health has been a vulgar error. Eating snow, however, does not quench thirst, but melted snow is as efficacious for this purpose as rain water. *Well water* is generally more impregnated with earthy salts, especially bicarbonate and sulphate of lime. Its hardness is shown by its curdling and decomposing soap, instead of mixing with it and readily forming suds, as can be noticed of soft water. Some country wells, however, have very good water, which fact, to a great extent, is governed by their healthful surroundings and by the geological formations of the grounds through which and under which their feeders travel to collect their storage. *River water* is an admixture of rain and spring water, and always holds in suspension a greater or less amount of extraneous matter, and in or around cities is strongly contaminated with decomposing animal and vegetable matters.

Much of our river water, however, as it runs through sparsely populated districts, is comparatively pure and healthful.

The Croton water of New York City contains a trifle over four grains of solid matter to the gallon, a grain and a half of this being carbonate of lime; the chlorides of calcium and magnesium and the carbonate of magnesia constitute a little over two grains.

The Cochituate water of Boston is about equally as pure, and the Schuylkill, of Philadelphia, nearly so.

The usual results of drinking hard waters, or those strongly impregnated with *cruriæ* of animal or vegetable substances, for any length of time, are dysenteries, protracted diarrhœa, and chronic affections of the kidneys. Previous to the introduction of the Croton River, the Manhattan water supplied to the citizens of New York contained, in some localities, 125 grains of different impurities to each gallon; in other parts, much less. Some of the wells in the lower part of that city contained from fifty to sixty grains to a gallon. The water in the wells of Boston, Philadelphia, and Cincinnati is in no better condition.

The waters of the Thames, in the vicinity of London, contain as impurities about twenty grains of solid matter to the gallon. Of this, carbonate of lime constitutes about sixteen grains, sulphate of lime and common salt about four grains.

The Ohio water at Cincinnati is of a fluctuating quality, but on an average compares favorably with either the Schuylkill or the Croton water. At its low stages, free ·ammonia can be more readily detected, and has been found as high as

11.5 in 1,000, while at its high stages its solids increase to from nine to fifteen grains to a gallon.

ADULTERATION OF WATER.

The purest water is liable to become impregnated with poisonous properties when conveyed through metallic pipes, particularly leaden ones. The air contained in strictly pure water rapidly corrodes lead; distilled water, from which the air is excluded, has no action on it until air is admitted again, when a thin white crust of carbonate and hydrate of the oxide of lead is promptly formed. Rain water is often impregnated from the lead of roofs, gutters, cisterns, and pipes. Combinations of lead, iron, and zinc, and other mixed metals, as in cases where iron bars are used to support leaden cisterns, the introduction of iron pumps into leaden cisterns, etc., often produce a galvanic action which dissolves a portion of the lead.

Chemists do not agree respecting the action of water drawn through leaden conduits, but experience settles this question affirmatively. It becomes our citizens, therefore, to exercise a constant watchfulness in its employment, which is to let as much water run as the leaden pipes contain to their junction with the iron pipes in the streets, before drinking it. These facts prove that the

principle of conveying water through our dwellings by leaden pipes is wrong, and a substitute
should engage the attention of sanitary engineers
and philanthropists.

PURIFICATION OF COMMON WATERS.

Filtration removes all *infusoria*, living *animal-
cula*, and suspended impurities, but it does not
deprive water of substances it holds in solution.
Boiling destroys the vitality of animal and vegetable substances it may contain, expels air or carbonic acid, and causes precipitation of carbonate
of lime. Sometimes it may be advantageous to
boil water first and filter it afterwards. Distillation
purifies water from everything except traces of
organic matter; it is, however, a process too trou-
blesome and expensive for general employment in
the household. An ordinary funnel made of, or
lined with, blotting paper, and half or one-third
filled with pulverized charcoal, makes a good filter.

A wholesome and the most agreeable temperature for drinking-water is from 50° to 55° F. A
further reduction by ice, especially in hot weather,
when freely indulged in becomes injurious.

MILK, CONSIDERED AS A DRINK AND AS AN ARTICLE OF DIET.

The milk of mammals, though an animal secretion, can hardly be called animal food, in strict

language. It contains, on the average, ninety per cent. of water and about ten per cent. of solid matter, consisting of butter, casein, sugar and various salts

Although milk cannot, of necessity, be considered a strictly natural food, except during the period of infancy, when the teeth are undeveloped,—and no animals of the mammalia class, save man, employ it otherwise,—it is, nevertheless, when pure, the best form of aliment out of the legitimate order of natural foods. It contains really all the elements requisite for prolonged nutrition, and, except in certain abnormal states of the digestive organs, its moderate employment is attended with no inconvenience. Some invalids do not enjoy it, some dyspeptics cannot tolerate it, but exceptional cases under morbid conditions are not the rules for healthy persons.

No secretion is so readily affected by the *ingesta* or the general health of the animal producing it as the milk. The taste, color, and odor of cow's milk are easily modified or influenced by the food. Children are frequently salivated, narcotized, catharticised, poisoned, and disordered in many ways, through the mother's milk. The organic instincts, true to the first principle of self-preservation, determine the accidental impurities of the body to this channel as the most ready way of expelling them from the body. Nursing mothers have little idea how much disease, pain, and misery they inflict on their little ones, nor how frequently they commit infanticide, by taking irritating aliments and drinks or injurious drugs into their own stomachs. This subject cannot be presented with too much force as to its bearing on the well-being of the human race. There should be a medical reformation in the way of dieting mothers and doctoring children.

The milk produced by cows fed on distillery slops, which, to the disgrace of municipal authorities, rich men are yet permitted to sell to the poor in some of our large cities, is not only very innutritious, but absolutely poisonous. These cows are kept in close and horribly filthy stables, fed on warm slops and other refuse matters of these establishments, which rot their teeth, weaken their limbs, and render their whole bodies masses of disease; and their milk is furnished to some of our citizens as an article of diet for their children.

Milk, in its normal or pure state, contains seventy-three nutritious parts in one thousand, but it is the only substance thoroughly prepared by nature as a ready nutriment, as it is essentially composed of three substances, namely, saccharine, olein, and casein, the last much similar to albumen. From this comparison we arrive at the conclusion that all nutriment for men and the higher order of animals might be brought back to these three standard substances. If we analyze and investigate them in all analogical forms, we find that the characteristic peculiarity of all sugary substances (saccharines) consists merely in their composition of carbon (thirty to fifty per cent.), with oxygen and hydrogen in the same proportion as they are found to compose water. The two other substances consist of compound bases (of which carbon forms the greater part), similarly mixed and modified by water. The proportion of carbon in oily substances (olein), which hold in this respect the first place, differs from about sixty to eighty per cent., and, therefore, if carbon is considered the measure of nutritive power, which in certain respects may be correct, then oils might be considered as the most nourishing substances. The general conclusion is, that those substances which by nature contain less than thirty or more than eighty per cent. of carbon, should not be used as an exclusive nutriment.

Now, if we inquire if animals could live exclusively on one single class of these three substances, we find that all trials have given testimony against such supposition, and the most acceptable view is, that a mixture of at least two of these nourishing substances, if not all three, is necessarily required. Milk is, therefore, such a compound, and all grasses and herbs which serve as food for animals contain at least two of the three substances found in milk. The same is true of all animal nutriment, which consists, at least, of albumen and oil. In short, it is perhaps impossible to name a substance used as nutriment by the higher order of animals which is not essentially and naturally composed of two, or all three, of these standard classes of nutritive substances.

In all our artificial nutriment we find most strictly this important principle of mixture. It seems to be the only purpose of all our labor exercised in the art of cookery, as little as we may be inclined to believe it. Thus has instinct taught man in early times to add butter or oil to mealy substances, like bread and others, by nature void of this matter. The same instinct has taught him to fatten animals in order to furnish oily substances mixed with albumen, which compound he consumes mixed up with saccharine, as contained in bread and vegetables. In fact, in his most chosen luxuries, in his most agreeable dainties, the same important principle is kept in view; in his sugar and fine flour, his eggs and butter, in all their various forms and compounds, are nothing but more or less hidden imitations and variations of the standard type of nutriment— the milk.

OF LIGHT.

The salutary and hygienic importance of light is not sufficiently understood by the people, nor its remedial influence properly regarded by physicians. Whether it be a distinct imponderable entity, a property of electricity, or something else, it would be idle here to speculate; but it is certain that the light which this earth derives from the sun and the fixed stars, has a powerful modifying influence on all the functions of its animal and vegetable kingdoms.

Some plants thrive best when exposed to strong sunlight, others in a moderate light, and others when considerably shaded; yet all of them, without exception, require a good degree of the influence of light to become hardy, firm, and vigorous. Those which grow in deeply shaded situations or dark cellars are comparatively colorless, slender, and friable. Light is the cause of color in all bodies; it is entirely reflected by white surfaces, and completely absorbed by black. Plants absorb carbon, and give out oxygen or vital air in the light, but during the night this process is reversed, so that they absorb oxygen

and give out carbon. Hence, it is injurious and
even dangerous to sleep at night in situations
closely surrounded with dense foliage, or in
rooms where flowers are kept in large quantities,
unless especially well ventilated.

The nutritive process is materially checked in
all vegetables and animals when deprived of light
for a considerable time; in this case vegetables
are said to become etiolated, a condition analo-
gous to that called *anæmia*, or *hyperæmia*, in man—
a state of debility, bloodlessness, or inanition.
In some of the lower animals the process of meta-
morphosis is arrested by deprivation of the solar
influence. The tadpole, instead of developing
into a frog, either continues to grow as a tadpole,
or degenerates into some kind of monstrosity;
fish in dark caverns are known to propagate without eyesight; and specimens of human monstros-
ities, developed abnormally, in consequence of
the absence of a due degree of Heaven's light,
are neither few nor far between in the under-
ground tenements of large cities. Almost the
entire population of our large cities who occupy
back rooms and rear buildings where the sun
never shines, and cellars and vaults below the
level of the ground on the shaded side of narrow
streets, are more or less diseased. Of those who
do not die of acute diseases, a majority exhibit

unmistakable marks of imperfect development and deficient vitality; and, in fact, as with animals and vegetables in like circumstances, often run into chronic debilities and deformities, not more reproachful, however, to those parents who rear families under such disadvantages, than disgraceful to that city, State, or national government which permits any class of its citizens to live in such abodes.

Light, then, and an abundant supply of it, is indispensable to a due development of all organized bodies. Medical practitioners have always observed that diseases of all kinds, from the most trifling toothaches, quinsy, or rheumatism, to the severest attack of fever, scrofula, or incipient stages of consumption, are much less manageable in low, dark apartments. And it is notorious that, during the prevalence of epidemics, the shaded side of narrow streets invariably exhibits the greatest ratio of fatal cases.

AIR AND SUN-BATHS.

Dr. Edwards, a noted writer on hygiene, observes that the influence of light in promoting the perfect development of animals, led him to conclude that in climates where nudity is not incompatible with health, exposure of the whole surface of the body to light is favorable to the

regular conformation of the body, and he, therefore, has suggested insolation in the open air and
solar light as a means calculated to restore
healthy confirmation to children affected with
scrofula, whose deviations of form do not appear
to be incurable.

Pereira remarks: "As in bright sunlight we
feel more active, cheerful, and happy, while
obscurity and darkness give rise to a gloomy and
depressed condition of mind, we may employ
insolation in the open air as a mental stimulus in
melancholy, lowness of spirits, and despondency."

The inferences deducible from the foregoing
reflections are sufficiently obvious. All persons,
in order to acquire and maintain the best conditions of health and strength, should be frequently
exposed to the light of the sun, except when
oppressively hot. Children are generally mal-
treated, more especially in cities, in being kept
almost entirely excluded from sunshine. Many
good mothers are more fond of delicate faces and
pale complexions of their little ones, than they
are intelligent in relation to their physiological
welfare. A little sun-browning occasionally of
their faces, necks, hands, and feet, or their whole
bodies, would not only render their development
more perfect and enduring, but tend to the production of the greatest symmetry and beauty in
manhood and womanhood.

Dwelling houses ought to be constructed with especial reference to light. Those rooms which are most occupied should always be the best lighted. The sun should be allowed free access to the yard and out-grounds. Shade trees and shrubbery, pleasant and useful to some extent, should never be so close as to shut the direct rays of the sun out entirely. The influence of light in dissipating and decomposing noxious vapors and deleterious gases, which collect in and around low grounds and dark places, is very great, and generally not fully appreciated.

OF SLEEP.

Sleep is the temporary interruption of all our relations with external objects—a complete repose of the organs of sense, intellectual faculties, and all voluntary motion. The constitutional relation of man to the changes of the seasons and the succession of days and nights, seems to imply the necessity of sleep. The time of sleep required by different individuals varies greatly, according to temperament, manner of life, dietetic habits, etc. John Wesley, with an active, nervous temperament, and a rigidly plain vegetable diet, could perform mental and bodily labors almost Herculean and sleep but four or five hours out of twenty-four, while Daniel Webster, with a more powerful but less active organization, and an ordinary mixed diet, had a talent for sleeping eight or nine hours.

Profound and quiet sleep means the perfect cessation of the functions referring to the cerebral hemispheres and the sensory ganglia, and is attended with entire unconsciousness. Dreaming implies imperfect rest, some disturbing cause. usually gastric irritation, exciting the brain to feeble and disordered functional action. Individuals of very studious habits, and those whose labors are disproportionally intellectual, require more sleep than those whose duties or pursuits require more manual and less mental exertion. But no avocation or habit affects this question so much as the quality of the *ingesta*. Physiologists are not well agreed respecting the natural duration of sleep. Historical data, however, seem to indicate that a great majority of those who attained remarkable longevity were good sleepers, averaging, probably, at least eight hours. Nature seems to invite us to retire soon after dark and to arise with the morning light. During the cold season, when the nights are longer, more sleep is required. For all those whose general habits of life are correct, and who retire at the proper time, from six to nine hours, if their slumber is quiet and sweet, may not be excessive.

Dreamy, restless dozing in the morning after sunrise, is more debilitating than refreshing.

The propriety or advantage of sleeping after meals, or after the principal meal at least, has been under discussion these many days. The dinner-nap has received more serious consideration *pro et con* than the importance surrounding it could possibly justify. It is well known that all the *mammalia* seek rest after a full meal. We would place this question under the general rule of Frederick the Great, cited in the chapter on Food. If the noon meal is partaken of during regular hours, between twelve and three o'clock, and at the same time is made the principal meal of the day, a complete rest thereafter for one or two hours may be very appropriate; and, if such time is merely spent in mental and physical passivity, pleasant and light conversation, easy, cheerful reading or a short nap, it matters little; the digestive process will pass with more comfort and be shorter than if we should rush things again right after arising from the table.

Our position during sleep should be perfectly flat, or horizontal, with the head slightly raised. One common-sized hair pillow is generally sufficient. A majority of people sleep with the head too high, often elevated on two thick pillows, with a heavy bolster in addition. The position thus assumed is a bad one; the neck is bent, the chest compressed, and the whole body unnaturally crooked. Some writers object to sleeping on the back, and assign as a reason that the stomach and other abdominal organs press upon the large blood-vessels below the heart, and thereby produce a tendency to cerebral disturbances, nightmare, apoplexy, etc. This argument has weight only with those who indulge in late or heavy suppers, or suffer from enlarged livers, or other abnormal conditions. Healthy persons of correct habits may sleep at pleasure on the back, or reclining to one side.

The nature of the beds and bedclothing are of importance to those who would preserve or attain good health. Feathers must be left out of all consideration; they should be excluded from every hygienic bedroom. Straw, corn-husks, hair, or clean and well-dried grasses, make comfortable and healthy beds. Wire spring-mattresses covered with a quilt, are still better. Children and infants are cruelly, though unwittingly, abused when compelled to sleep on feathers. The bedclothes should be as light as possible, consistent with comfort. Linen or cotton sheets are better than flannel blankets next to the body. Thin quilts are best in summer, with an additional blanket or two during winter months.

Of bedrooms and their management otherwise, we have spoken in the chapter on Air.

CONCLUSION.

We have, in the foregoing chapters, presented the broad outlines of Hygiene in its general and most important bearing upon the welfare of man, as far as the space of this volume would permit. For some subdivisions,—on heating of dwellings, the proper temperatures thereof, controlling passions, the reform of bad habits, hygienic cookery, etc.,—we refer the reader to numerous special works on those subjects. We cannot, however, dismiss this theme without appealing to the honor and good sense of all in whose hands this little work should find its way to beware of the mischief and degradation involved by becoming

SLAVES TO TOBACCO.

It is the worst of our "national sins," and is sapping the life-blood and stunting the growth of our youths this very day. It is ruinous; it has no redeeming feature whatever. Its very bad influence is manifest at the occasion when tempted to make the first experiment. It is a poison, and makes its novices deadly sick. Snuffing is worse than smoking; chewing is worse than snuffing, and of smoking, that of the cigarette is the superlative of all that is loathsome and disgusting; not only because in its manufacture one poison is added to another,—opium to nicotine,—but also on account of the well-known fact that all refuse of tobacco and the stumps of cigars, collected from the street, out of the gutters, and the spittoons of the hotels, are utilized in its production. These collections have become a regular industry of our "street arabs" in all the large cities.

The prevalence of cigarette smoking has been of late greatly on the increase, and the use of this narcotic compound commences with the young from mere childhood. Such a habit can not be more lamented than reprobated. The injury done to the constitution of the young may not immediately appear, but cannot fail ultimately to become a great national calamity. The very difficulty of learning to smoke, or to to chew, should be evidence of its danger. The headache, nausea, and vertigo with which it is acquired, should be sufficient to show that the habit is most injurious, and only made endurable by long and frequent experiments

Constant, private secretary, furnishes the following account of an attempt of the first Napoleon: "He once took a fancy to smoke for the purpose of trying a very fine Oriental pipe, presented to him by a Turkish ambassador. After it was lighted for him, he contented himself with opening and shutting his mouth alternately, without once drawing in his breath. 'How the d——,' cried he at last, 'It does nothing!' I made him observe the reason of his failure, and showed him the proper mode of doing. But scarcely had he drawn in a mouthful when the smoke, which he knew not how to expel, turned back into his palate, penetrated into his throat, came out by his nose, and blinded him. As soon as he recovered,—'Take that away from me!' 'What abomination!' 'Oh, the swine!' 'My stomach turns!' In fact, he was sick, and felt himself so annoyed that he renounced forever the 'pleasure' which, he said, 'was only fit to amuse sluggards.'"

James, "by the grace of God, King of Great Britain," on July 5, 1616, finds it proper to publish his "Counterblast to Tobacco." "In my opinion," says the royal commentator, "there cannot be a more base and yet more hurtful corruption in a country than the vile use of tobacco." After enumerating the many evils emanating therefrom, he concludes as follows: "A custom loathsome to the eye, hateful to the nose, harmful to the brain, dangerous to the lungs, and, in the black stinking fume thereof, nearest resembling the horrible Stygian smoke of the pit that is bottomless."

Yet to this day, at the close of the great nineteenth century, we notice a wonderful ignorance of the public regarding the nature of tobacco. Even intelligent, well-educated men stare in astonishment when you tell them that tobacco is one of the most powerful poisons we possess. The medical profession, we are sorry to observe, has been trifling with the subject, or, what is worse still, the majority of its members encourage the habit by their own example. We most earnestly desire to see the habit of using tobacco in any form diminish, and we entreat the youth of this country to abandon it altogether. Let them lay our advice to heart and give up a dubious pleasure for a certain good!

WILL IN DISEASE.

"After a hundred years of history and education in scientific medicine, and in a country where shrewd common sense has been developed in the most backward-looking mind, at such time, and under such circumstances, it would have seemed impossible that the incurable sick, the paralyzed, and the maimed should, by thousands, flock to a priest to be cured of their diseases. The newspapers say the immense depot at Pittsburgh has of late seemed like a hospital, filled as it has been with the poor unfortunate invalids seeking Father

Mollinger's supernatural aid to make them well.
The father anoints and blesses, and the young
man who 'had not walked since childhood,' upon
command, goes unassisted 'from the altar-rail to
the rear of the church, to the amazement of the
vast audience.' Though the report says the
great majority are sadly disappointed,—even the
squarely impossible cannot be done in these
times,—a number are found that, with functional
affections, under strong emotions, exhibit a change,
or an increase of strength, so that the belief in
the power is kept living.

"What is it that makes Father Mollinger's
Christian science, faith-cure, medical spiritualism,
etc., possible in the nineteenth century? Were
there absolutely no element of truth in these
reported cures, even the dullest dupe would come
at last to some consciousness of the *modus
operandi*. The manure of the soil nourishing
these delusions is a truth too often ignored and
neglected by scientific medicine. It is the truth
of the power of the emotions, of the will, of the
spirit, if you please, over the flesh; of life over
the beginnings of disease, and even over disease
and death itself. Races and nations differ greatly
in their power of resisting and overcoming
disease, simply by reason of the characteristic
attitude of the will and the disposition of the

11

patient toward the physical illness. Just so do all, even brothers, differ in the same way. Thousands are physically sick because mental resolution and spiritual domination are weak and illogical. This is strikingly true in reference to the beginnings of disease.

"The secret of continuous good health does not always consist merely in physical resistance or robustness, but in sharply conquering the subtle beginnings of corporeal abnormity by pure will-power. There are two homologues of this power that illustrate it exactly. Who has not seen whimsicality, crankiness, and oddity by self-indulgence slowly degenerate into monomania, and even into downright insanity? And again, who can doubt that in the commencement many such persons are perfectly conscious of the abnormal tendency, and are, moreover, perfectly capable of not doing the ridiculous or self-forgetful things? They are, at first, driven by no imperious necessity. It is precisely so when one gives way to immoral courses of life. At first, the voice of conscience is clear; by and by, control is lost and the voice is entirely silent. The analogies obtain in the matter of health. The adage, 'Resist the beginnings of evil,' holds also here. All disease begins subtly, almost insensibly; a chill, lassitude, *malaise*, etc., caught at this stage and fought **down by** virile volition, that which by self-indulgence would have proceeded to genuine fever and illness, may often be resolved into routine normality of health. A brisk walk of five miles in the teeth of exhaustion and weariness has saved many from severe illness. And so in types of disease that are, if one may so express it, more organic. The fact cannot be disputed that many who have believed themselves incapable of walking, under powerful emotion, their own will being supplemented and 'relayed' by that of another, do really find that they can walk a little. Our confutation of the priests' supernaturalism consists precisely in this proved power of the will. Doubtless orthopedic appliances are often given patients who need only resolution, encouragement, and repeated trial in order to develop, by exercise, what the crutch really conceals, or neutralizes. In the sick room every experienced practitioner knows how much depends upon the *morale*, the resolution of the patient, and how even death and life may depend upon the will. All this, when we read it, seems trite enough, but its significance is lost sight of in the battle of rival theories of disease, and to some it must seem the froth of nonsense. But the practical lesson of the very obvious truth consists in the simple

duty of arousing the will to self-confidence and
corporeal domination. As has been well demonstrated, the best cure for the most outrageous
hysteria is mental and volitional control, sup-
planting the patient's diseased imagination by a
healthy one—true faith-cure in a legitimate and
genuine sense. The puppets of fashionable auto-
matonism are prone to run to the doctor for
every ache, real or suspected. To indulge them
in their folly sometimes seems to the physician
not without a certain worldly excuse. But if a
higher ethical ruling is adhered to, duty will
counsel encouragement of *prophylaxis* and hygiene; and among the means of forefending
disease, an energetic domination of will over the
body is often the most vital and important."[1]

"'You must have that blister on, or you will
die,' said her physician to the redoubtable Sarah,
first Duchess of Marlborough, when suffering
from pleurisy. 'I will not have a blister on, and
I will not die,' said the indomitable Sarah. And
she did neither. The woman who mastered John
Churchill and Anne Stuart was not going to suc-
cumb to a pleurisy! And in disease the influence
of the will is as potent as elsewhere. It cannot
rescue a person from the clutch of a mortal
malady; but if the disease is compatible with

[1] *Medical News*, July, 1891.

recovery, the will makes the difference, often, betwixt death and life.

"When Douglas Jerrold was once at death's door, and his physician told him he must die, his answer was: 'What, and leave a family of helpless children? I won't die!' and die he did not, at least not at that time. A strong motive to live positively keeps some people alive, as it did with Douglas Jerrold. The will stands in some curious relations to health, or rather disturbances of health. The cases of imaginary diseases which rest casually upon disorder of the will or morbid manifestation of will, seen outside of asylums, are not rare. They occur mostly in young women, usually those who may be said to be of a nervous constitution. Sometimes the patient is highly intelligent; at other times the nervous system is but imperfectly developed. Be that as it may, a disorder of the will takes place, and this in turn starts some bodily malady in which it finds expression. Sometimes there is loss of speech, sometimes there is paralysis, may be of the legs, may be of one limb; or, the patient declares her inability to get up from her bed, as not unfrequently happens with not very strong-minded girls after an unsuccessful love affair, or the young female declines to eat, like the Welsh fasting girl.

"The malady is not hysterical, though possessing many features in common with hysteria. The friends are greatly alarmed at first, but a reaction usually sets in. If the relatives continue very sympathizing, the malady will persist. *Hypochondriasis* is another morbid state where the will is in abeyance. Of insanity and the will little can be said here. In many cases it seems as if the patient had but to make an effort to throw off the incubus, the impression which predominates him or her. But then the patient just cannot make that effort any more than Dickens' dying lady, and

> lies widowed
> Of the power which bows the will.'

"Whether persistent attention directed to any one part and long maintained ever ends in actual disease of the said part, may not be affirmed. It is a matter to which systematic attention has not yet been paid. On the contrary, many cures can only be explained by the mental impression the material agent employed has made, and through the mind the body is reached. 'Conceit can kill and conceit can cure,' is a quaint old saying as to the effect of faith in remedies in some morbid conditions.

"The will in acute diseases is in many cases most potent. If the patient has no strong motive to live, the struggle is soon over, the resistance is feeble. This is a well-known matter in medical practice. If a sick person really ill becomes convinced that the grave is the only prospect, the desired result is almost always brought about. Where there exists a strong motive to live, no matter whether selfish or unselfish, a successful struggle is often the result. Aaron Burr, when a young man, 'laid aside a wasting disease like a garment' in order to join Arnold on his raid against Quebec, and a very arduous undertaking it was.

"The question of will in relation to the progress of disease is constantly met with in medical practice. On the other hand, given a woman of ardent temperament with sufficient motive to live, and nothing but mortal disease can kill her. . . . . The effect of disease upon the will is curious. The consumptive is sanguine to the last, often even when death is impending. The cancerous patient meets death with a sullen defiance; the pyæmic patient, after the first long shivering fit, maintains an attitude of indifference. In chronic diseases, certain mental relations of bodily maladies can be traced. Where there has been habitual long depression, the spirits become permanently lowered; the past can never be erased out of the memory. The brain, long ill-fed with blood, will take an habitually gloomy view of everything. All is painted in with India ink, and it is most difficult to dispel the gloom. When the liver is upset, the brain is poisoned with toxic 'liver stuffs' and melancholy (literally, 'black bile,' in Greek) is the result.

> "'The yellow gall that in your bosom floats,
> Engenders all these melancholy thoughts,'

wrote Dryden, who perhaps had some bitter personal experience on the subject. Even a very firm will is taxed to bear up under such bodily conditions, and appropriate measures for bodily relief may be resorted to with advantage. 'Talk of champagne,' wrote Byron, 'for clearing your thoughts! There is nothing like Epsom salts.' The 'bilious' are rarely hopeful; as a class they are a depressed race, though often tenacious of purpose. Just so, gout creates a mental condition of irritability blended with depression, as Sydenham describes. A 'gouty brain' is a legitimate expression, and we can no more expect a brain poisoned with gout to work smoothly than we can expect an elastic tread with a gouty foot. For brain, 'as the organ of mind,' is affected by bodily conditions. What says Dr. Richardson, who first made clear certain affection of the heart? 'The man or woman with a hesitating heart is thereby unfitted for sudden tasks, demands,

resolves, which, when the heart is firm, are considered of little moment, for when the heart
hesitates, the brain, which reposes for its power
on the blood the heart supplies to it, falters with '
the heart, just as the gas flickers when the steady
pressure is taken off the main. From these circumstances some persons, who once were known
as resolute and determined, lose those qualities
when they are subjected to intermittent action of
the heart, becoming, as their friends say, uncertain and doubtful in character; becoming, as they
themselves feel and know, less the masters of
themselves and less secure in their own work,
and skill and power.'

"We use the term 'stout-hearted' and 'faint-
hearted' in secret acknowledgment of the relations of the brain 'as an organ of mind' to the
vigor of the heart. The Hebrew priest was
ordered to approach the Israelitish host when
going into battle. 'And shall say unto them,
Hear, O Israel: ye approach this day unto battle
against your enemies: let not your hearts faint,
fear not, and do not tremble, neither be ye terrified
because of them.' And what is good for the
Israelites going into battle is good for men
inclining to falter when fighting the battle of life.
A faint-hearted person is not likely to be successful in any arduous undertaking; in one matter, at

least, there is a proverb to this effect: 'Faint heart never won fair lady.' In courtship, courage is requisite if the fair one be coy; and no woman in the world was ever won by a man who lacked courage,—though she may possibly consent to marry him.

"There are other bodily conditions than a hesitating heart where the will is broken. Long continued wearing battle with circumstances saps the will-power of all except those who possess it in its highest development. It is not every one who can snatch success out of defeat, as Napoleon did at Marengo. Robert Bruce found himself much sustained by the spider's performance, in his later efforts against the dominant English, and wrenched Scotland from the grip of the Norman-English at last. When the will fails the battle is lost. When a man feels he can no longer bear up, or make further effort, he is worsted.

"It is impossible to conclude this subject without a few words about the effect of toxic agents upon the will-power, especially alcohol and chloral hydrate. The effect of long indulgence in alcohol is to enfeeble the mind. The chronic drunkard exhibits a childish range of thought in one case; in another, an impish malice, which, fortunately, is only held in check by that intense disinclination to act common with chronic alcoholism. It is, usually, not difficult to fire him to a resolution when under the exhilarating effect of drink; but when the drink is dead in him, the will goes with it. Macaulay says of the Jacobite plotters against the life of William III.: 'It was universally remarked that the malcontents looked wiser than usual when they were sober, and bragged more than usual when they were drunk.' And of Preston, who was in the tower under sentence of death for being concerned in a Jacobite plot, he says: 'He was informed that his fate depended on himself. The struggle was long and severe. Pride, conscience, party spirit, were on one side, the intense love of life on the other. He went, during a time, irresolutely to and fro. He listened to his brother Jacobites, and his courage rose. He listened to the agents of the government, and his heart sank within him. On an evening, when he had dined and drank his claret, he feared nothing. He would die like a man rather than save his neck by an act of baseness. But his temper was very different when he woke the next morning, when the courage he had drawn from wine and company had evaporated, when he was alone with iron gates and stone walls, when the thought of the block, the axe, and the sawdust rose in his mind. During some time, he regularly wrote a confession every fore-

noon when he was sober, and burned it every
night when he was merry.'

"So it is with the chronic drunkard, only in a
more pronounced degree. He is always bragging
of what he will do, or might have done; he is in
the potential mood — might, could, or would — and
never in the indicative mood, except as to the
future tense,—never as to the past tense. He is
misleading, not always by design, but because he
misleads himself first and others after. Irreso-
lution is his characteristic, except as to selfishness and his immediate wants.

"Then, as to the effects of chloral hydrate, the
misuse of which is, unfortunately, so very common
at the present time. The sleepless person secretly
drinks a draught of chloral, and gains the coveted
sleep, but at what cost! The chloral puts the brain
to sleep, partly by direct action upon it, partly by
reducing the amount of blood going to it; and
the latter condition tends to persist. Consequently, the persons who slept on chloral find
the brain the next day unequal to its best efforts;
the blood pressure on the brain cannot be worked
up as before, and a horrid sense of lethargy, in
time, settles upon the individual. Less work is
done, but by greater effort; the will is impaired,
and again impotence is stealing on. These two
toxic enemies of the will-power are responsible

for an immensity of ill around us at the present day. * * *

"The moral of it all is that the will may cut two ways—for good or for evil, towards making angels or devils. Mighty as the will is, the first numeral in character, the next is principle in this world. In the next world, we are told, principle will come first. The will may become itself diseased, as in the case of Napoleon, in the individual; it may become diseased nationally, as was the case in Italy, under Pope Alexander VI., in the sixteenth century, and to a less extent in Spain. There is, then, will in disease and will in health; the first productive of evil,—'Woe unto those by whom offenses come'; the other, the spirit which moves the individual to efforts which, in time, enable him to attain success, often to become the benefactor of his race."[1]

We will conclude this chapter by referring to and adding one of the most striking illustrations of its general philosophy in the history of our present time. A few years ago, General U. S. Grant, in robust health, at an age when many men of his even and easy temperament might have enjoyed yet two or more decades of natural life, was suddenly attacked by a most pernicious malignant disease. He knew it would cut short his time on

[1] "Will Power," by J. Milner Fothergill, M. D.

earth, his physicians had calculated for him on its limit; but, like Douglas Jerrold, he was not quite ready to part with those he loved. He was then engaged in writing his "Memoirs," the proceeds of which were to add to the comfort of those dearest and nearest to him, after his departure. The same characteristic which distinguished him at Fort Donelson and before the walls of Vicksburg, came to his rescue; the same great self-possession, combined with a powerful will for good, never failed him. He finished his book with grim Death knocking at the door every day, but not until it was done did he give up the struggle, and for the first time "surrendered."

From his invincible will Wellington was spoken of as the "Iron Duke," and well he deserved the name. Men with marked will-power have come to the front in emergencies, as seen in Oliver Cromwell and Napoleon. In both these instances, as in that of Grant, national convulsions produced the seething caldron, from whence they rose to an eminence of position and fame. But when we consider the relations of this power of will to the other qualities, the next and most important is the amount of *principle* to be found with the will. Both Napoleons were bad men. Napoleon the First was a villain; "Napoleon the Little" was a self-made emperor, too, but with it all he was

only a disreputable scoundrel. With the Napoleons, patriotism was nothing; selfishness and
ambition everything. With Oliver Cromwell,
George Washington, and Ulysses Grant the case
stands reversed.

HYGIENE IN MATRIMONY.

We have, during the last half of the present
century, observed great progress and improvements in the propagation of horses, cattle, sheep,
and other domestic animals. Men study the different strains and the effect of their combination;
they import new blood from every quarter of the
globe to advance in value and excellence these
useful animals. Crossbreeding and proper selection for this purpose has become a science. What
are the facts and conditions relating to these
highly important features when applied to the
human family? Total consternation, ignorance,
and corruption everywhere. Society allows an
inveterate, chronic drunkard, or half idiot, to
marry, if he is "of age," regardless of consequences. Society witnesses the same sacred rite
between a criminal just out of the penitentiary,
and a lewd woman, maybe tainted with disease,
without the least apprehension. Where will this
lead to, and whither are we drifting? The day
must come when the responsibility will have to

be placed somewhere. A license board, of which one member should be an experienced surgeon, one a lawyer, and the other three men of high moral training—the heads of families—and all appointed by the mayor, with rules laid down by a medical council, could do much to protect a community from certain moral and physical contamination

In Sparta, as Plutarch tells us, immediately after the birth of a child, it was taken from its mother and carried to a place called *lésche*, where the heads of different families, constituting a council, were assembled to examine the infant. If well-formed and robust, its limbs properly shaped, without visible indications of disease, it was decided that it should be brought up; but if it was deformed, ugly, feeble, or exhibiting predisposition to physical disorders, it was condemned to be thrown into a place vulgarly called *apothetis;* as it was considered inexpedient that any child should live, unless likely to become a vigorous and useful citizen. While we are far from recommending the laws of ancient Sparta to be applied to our present society, a wiser and more humane court should hold its session to deliberate upon the best manner of *preventing* the birth of feeble, diseased, or deformed children.

A similar code for the salvation and the continuance of physical power, strength, and endurance, has been in force among the Patagonians for many hundred years, and that it is exercised in some degree at the present time can hardly be contradicted. Dr. Oswald, in his series of "International Health Studies," published by Dr. J. H. Kellogg, at Battle Creek, Michigan, in the *Journal of Hygiene*, refers to a report of the great traveler Guinnard. That report, he says, confirmed by the statements of subsequent explorers, makes it probable that the main explanation of the Patagonian puzzle[1] can be found in the result of a thorough and merciless system of artificial selection, practiced through a long course of many generations. About three weeks after childbirth, Patagonian mothers submit their infants to the inspection of the Sachem of the tribe, who decides the youngster's fitness for survival by traditional rules, and in about three out of ten cases concludes that the welfare of the community requires a veto of the maternal prayer. Misshapen and puny babies, and often children of weak mothers, or of parents already overburdened with progeny, are carried to the next ravine and abandoned to the beasts of the wilderness. Dr. Oswald remarks that, when Guinnard at last solved the secret,—that of their

[1] Puzzle refers to their great size and vigor.

12

superior physique,—it was found that civilized nations must, on the whole, renounce the hope of profiting by its application.

It is the common consent of the medical world that libertines, drunkards, and gluttons cannot have healthy children, but we should trace the sources of these infirmities beyond their grosser manifestations. Neither the father whose nerves are shattered by tobacco and alcohol, whose digestion is disordered by improper food, whose constitution is impaired by drug medication, or whose blood is inflammatory with the violence of ungoverned passions, nor the mother whose muscular system is enfeebled, whose nerves are debilitated, or whose abdominal organs are contracted and rigid, and whose brain is constantly irritated by indolence, novel reading, constipating food, strong coffee, green tea, or the frequent indulgence of a morbid and fretful mood, can do justice to the rising generation. In this way do the sins of the fathers and mothers curse their own offspring through many generations.

In a very excellent work by Ira Mayhew, the author remarks: "Physiologists in general coincide in the belief that a vigorous and healthy physical and mental constitution in the parents communicates existence in the most perfect state to their offspring; while impaired constitutions, from whatever cause, are transmitted to posterity. In this sense, all who are competent to judge are agreed that the "Giver of life is a jealous God, visiting the iniquity of the fathers upon the children unto the third and fourth generation." Strictly speaking, it is not disease which is transmitted so often, but organs of such imperfect structure that they are unable to perform their functions properly, and so weak as to be easily put into a morbid state of abnormal condition by causes which unimpaired organs would be able to resist.

Ample statistical data have settled the question that the first children of those who marry very young are more of animal propensities and less of the moral and intellectual than those born nearer the middle period of the life of the parents. Extensive observation has also established the position that a great majority of men and women, morally and intellectually eminent, have been among the younger children of the family. The elevation and improvement of the race, therefore, seems to be adversely affected by too early marriages. The soundest physiological writers regard twenty-one to twenty-five for the female, and twenty-five to thirty for the male, as the most appropriate ages for assuming the serious duties, as well as participating in the pleasures, of matrimonial life.

Nothing is more firmly established than the fact that the character and quality of the organization of the child are seriously dependent on that of both parents, and this fact is of immense importance in its bearings on the well-being of the great family of mankind. Though the principle is generally well understood, it is much overlooked in theory and disregarded in practice. It is a matter of astonishment that even the standard works on physiology and obstetrics, as used in our medical schools of the present day, never elucidate the subject thoroughly—seldom allude to it. But let it be well understood by all who contemplate the matrimonial relations, as well as those who enjoy them already, that precisely according to the development, purity, and vigor of their own bodily and mental conditions, will be the physiological integrity and mental character of their offspring. It should be known, too, that the passion which impels to procreation, lying at the very foundation of vital existence, is of necessity one of the most powerful of the propensities; and that, while its rational and legitimate exercise is conducive to health, moral purity, and intellectual vigor, its excessive indulgence or abuse is as conducive to functional enervation and moral corruption.

The best authors are divided on the question,

whether organizations similar or unlike are most conducive to vigorous offspring. The majority maintain that temperaments, complexions, etc., decidedly different and opposite, make the most fortunate alliances for the offspring; and the same principle is held in relation to the mental standard. This proposition is strongly corroborated by the favorable results of cross breeding in different animals, and even from the cross marriages of the people of mixed nationalities, so far as observations have been recorded. When both parties are healthfully developed, however, in body and mind, actively engaged in some occupation which gives free exercise to all the functions and faculties, all habits being at the same time physiologically correct, congenial temperaments, will not, as a rule, be detrimental.

STIRPICULTURE.[1]

"A systematic and carefully executed experiment in human stirpiculture was made at the Oneida Community, in central New York, from 1868 to 1879. To explain how this came to pass requires some account of the man who planned the experiment and of the path which led to its inception and partial consummation.

"John Humphrey Noyes was born in Southern

[1] Webster's definition of *Stirpiculture:* "The breeding of special stock or races."

Vermont in 1811. Of strongly religious inheritance and training, he was also possessed of a logical and independent intellect. While a student of divinity at Yale in 1834, he originated and preached certain doctrines not in accord with Congregational tenets, which caused his expulsion from the church. We omit the various theories on which Noyes founded his new sect. Suffice it to state that, in consequence of their desired freedom from sin, the adherents of his doctrines are called Perfectionists. He himself says: 'Love in the exclusive form has jealousy for its complement, and jealousy brings on strife and division. Association, therefore, if it retains one-love-exclusiveness, contains the seeds of dissolution, and those seeds will be hastened to their harvest by the warmth of associate life.' He argued from the Bible that in the kingdom of heaven there is no marriage, since marriage is, like slavery, a form of selfish personal ownership; and to overcome this selfishness among perfectionists, Noyes devised an extraordinary system of regulated promiscuity, beginning at the earliest puberty, and by a method of his own invention he separated the amative from propagative functions. By this community of possession and of person he sought to root selfishness forever from the hearts of his disciples.

"The first feature was practiced on a small scale beginning 1841; the second, 'complex marriage' was inaugurated in 1846; but the other inhabitants of the New England village refused to view matters in a lenient light, and they showed their sentiments in no uncertain manner. Having left their home in consequence of this, the growing sect established itself in 1848 with some of Noyes's adherents, who lived near Oneida, New York. At the close of this year, the Oneida Community included eighty-seven persons. The succeeding year it doubled its numbers. Financial success was, of course, its first necessity, and twenty years of hard labor and earnest effort brought prosperity. The membership during this time was carefully limited, so that, in 1869, it had increased only to about two hundred and fifty. Previous to this date it was deemed desirable, for financial and other reasons, to restrict the birth-rate also. New members, of course, brought their children with them, but only two or three were born in the community each year. So well under control was this matter that only about one birth in eighteen months was accidental. The remaining births were from mothers who, for personal reasons, had obtained permission to increase the population of the community.

"Now, all this time Noyes was the leader and

the undisputed head, who, by his personal power and attraction, had drawn together, and kept together, this group of people, but the great object of his creed, namely, salvation from sin, disease, and death, could not wholly be accomplished in one lifetime. Therefore, the immediate necessities being obtained, it was to the future and the next generation that Noyes now turned his attention. It was a self-evident matter to him that for the attainment of his object, each generation must surpass the preceding one in holiness, and to accomplish this he devised the method of 'Stirpiculture' practiced by the community. Its first principle, founded on stock-raising experience, was that of a judicious in-and-in breeding, with frequent mingling of foreign blood.

"Since this stirpicultural experiment only produced one generation, the principle had but a limited application. The founder himself had eight children after he was fifty-eight years old, and among his adult relations in the community were his brother, his two sisters, and their children, with his own son, born before the community began.

"The second principle enunciated, which chiefly concerns us here, was that of careful selection of individuals for breeding purposes. Genealogies were studied, and medical histories compiled. A committee, headed by Noyes, took charge of the matter, and selected the holiest members who were free from physical defects. Intellectual and other considerations were given less weight, though in the later years physique and intellect were equally given their due place. The parents were of all ages, averaging as under ordinary circumstances, but the father was always older than the mother. One essential consideration was quite noteworthy. This was the mutual attraction which must exist, to at least a slight degree, between persons mated. Again, it some-times happened that a proposition would come from the individuals concerned, and if no objections were found, such requests were granted.

"The children born of this experiment between 1869 and 1879, inclusive, were sixty in number. Of these, only five died at, or near, birth, from unforeseen causes depending upon the mother. The remaining fifty-five were brought up with great care and under the best conditions until 1880, at which time they were from a few months to eleven years old. The infants were cared for exclusively by their mothers until nine months of age, and were nursed by them whenever possible; from then, and nine months longer, the mother had charge at night only, while after that age her individual responsibility for the child ceased. The children's department, whither it was now transferred, was managed by those persons who had shown themselves best fitted for the work, and was in a house apart from the large community building.

"In 1878 a 'Report on the Health of Children in the Oneida Community,' was published by Dr. Theodore R. Noyes, son of the founder. In this it was stated that serious sickness was unknown, and that the mortality at birth and up to nine years was less than one-third that of the United States at large, as given in the census. This difference is, however, partly due to the excellent sanitation, the protection from infection, and the other favorable post-natal conditions. The same may be said of the table comparing weight and height of these children with those of the Boston schools. Of nineteen of the former, then five to nine years old, all but one exceeded the Boston average in height, and all but four in weight also. The one weak member of this group was a boy who was deficient in coordinating power over his muscles, the only marked failure of the experiment.

"Dr. Noyes, in his report, draws the following conclusions: 'First, a little common sense applied to the mating of men and women for propagation must largely increase the proportion of viable children born; second, a viable child, once past the perils due to its mother, is nearly sure to grow up free from checks to its growth, under sanitary conditions, as good as those now prevailing in the community.' Yet it is evident that pre-natal culture did not lessen the need of post-natal care, for these experimenters knew that the eyes of the world were upon them, and, moreover, they believed that the future of the community rested with them. But alas!

" ' The best laid plans o' mice and men gang aft aglee.'

"Stirpiculture was planned to insure the future of the church and of the community; stirpiculture destroyed both

"Complex marriage, practiced by earnest, hardworking people, had held its own for twenty years. Selfish love, the loving of one person instead of the whole group, had been condemned and suppressed in every way, and so long as promiscuity could be enforced the effort was successful.

"But now one-fourth of the adult communists had been living in pairs for weeks or months, and these pairs had children; and there arose the unexpected issue—the spirit of monogamy—which now grew and spread until the whole body was infected with it. Success in business and leisure gave time for expressions of dissatisfaction; a discordant element found its way into the community; the old solidarity was gone, and each desired a mate.

"Noyes himself was weighed down with advancing years and deafness, and seeing before him the failure of all his hopes, he retired from the community. On August 26, 1879, the Oneida Community was assembled to consider a message from its founder, proposing that, 'in deference to public sentiment,' complex marriage should be renounced and ordinary marriage, or celibacy, substituted. A full vote was polled, and only three members opposed the proposition. Those who had been married before entering the community, twenty-five couples in all, were again husband and wife, and twenty marriages between individuals not previously wedded, took place within four months after the abandonment of the stirpicultural experiment. At this time two hundred and ninety-nine persons belonged to this society, comprising eighty-three children under twenty years, and two hundred and sixteen adults.

"Certain results of this experiment in human stirpiculture, probably the most systematic and extensive of modern times and by civilized peoples, are displayed by the children born under its conditions. In weighing the result, it should be remembered that the status of these children represents the product of two factors which cannot be separated, that is, the selection of parents; and second, community care and training of the young. This blending of causes was clearly recognized by Dr. Noyes. As he states it in the report referred to: 'The abolition of natural selection, by doing away with the vicissitudes which the strong alone can survive in childhood, must certainly lower the tone of adult health, unless artificial selection takes its place.' In point of fact, this artificial selection was so successful that the only death which occurred among the children of stirpiculture since 1880 was that of a boy, reared in spite of weakness, who succumbed to a trifling malady at about sixteen years of age.

"Speaking only of the older children, now twenty-two years old and under, the pride taken by the experimenters in their offspring is certainly warranted. The boys are tall, several over six feet, broad-shouldered and finely proportioned; the girls are robust and well built. Intellectually, both sides are of superior average. It is a surprise to find that little interest is taken by these young people in the peculiar circumstances of their origin, and that in spite of their early doctrinal training, a very few are church members, and but one is a perfectionist."

The above extract is from a paper read before the American Science Association, at Washington, August, 1891, by Anita Newcomb McGee, and can be found in full reprint in this year's (1892) January number of the *Herald of Health*, edited by Dr. M. L. Holbrook, New York.

John Humphrey Noyes died April 13, 1886, and with him ended a remarkable and interesting history.

The coöperative industry of the old concern, we believe, is still flourishing under the management of a stock company, chartered November, 1880, the stock being in the hands of seventy-five or one hundred of the old members.

While we would seriously hesitate to subscribe to the theories and forms under which these experiments were inaugurated, the lesson presented by their sequence is certainly important, and should ever be retained for valuable reflection.

CONFINEMENT MADE SAFE AND EASY.

With the introduction of many so-called modern improvements in our domestic economy, we have innocently adapted other changes without serious reference to their expediency. It is now considered almost a natural arrangement to have a physician engaged, often several months in advance, to attend and be present at the bedside of the prospective mother, and, Oh, "*horribile dictu*," the papers will have it: "Thanks to Doctor So-and-so," etc., just as if the proceedings of childbirth were looked upon as a violent disease or a dangerous operation, while in ninety-nine cases out of a hundred an intelligent physician will have very little or nothing to do but to let nature proceed in her own wise course. The less he assists, the better for the mother; his principal duty should be to keep others from meddling, and he should then be "thanked" all the more.

The original natives of this great Western Continent, the Indians, have precisely the same anatomical organization, governed by the same physiological laws, as their Caucasian cousins and successors. Their tribes are known to favor long tramps; their squaws are great walkers and good riders; they never stay at home on account of "interesting circumstances." When nature over-takes them, they stroll sideways in the bushes, attend to their own obstetrics, often unaided, and resume their march soon thereafter to rejoin the main column with their future chief or "princess" snugly put away on their backs or on the side of their saddle. We do not refer to this, however, without due sympathy for the squaw, because, in cases as above described, different and better conditions may often be desirable and of benefit to mother and child; yet, with these illustrations, and the facts substantially true, before us, we may obtain a lesson to lead us to the golden medium. Physical exercise, under favorable circumstances, up to the last day, is essential, and positively promotes a short and healthful performance of the most important act in female affairs.

It is but natural that conception and pregnancy, even in robust and otherwise healthy persons, bring about some marked changes, affecting the whole organization, the nervous system, the mind, and especially the digestive apparatus. The stomach becomes capricious, rejecting food which at other times it favors, and craves things indifferent or unnatural, often calling for sour, tart, or piquant eatables. Every organ becomes more or less crowded, the liver irritated, the bladder compressed, requiring more frequent attention. The breasts increase in size and become sensitive; the general irritation and excitement of the nervous system create new aches and pains; they also often cause aversion or a dislike, alternating with increased and stronger affection, toward the husband, etc. All these symptoms and changed feelings have their natural causes, and require no medicinal interference. Pregnancy is not a dis-

ease, but a glorious, healthful performance, and
in its normal progress, most independent of all
artificial improvements or assistance.   Abortion
and premature labor are the only serious and painful disorders to guard against.   The common
causes are local debility, violent mental agitation,
or bodily shocks and injuries.   Leucorrhœa and
excessive sexual indulgence will also produce
these conditions.   To deal of diseases of pregnancy as some of our medical publications do,
as a specialty, is absurd.   It is a well-known fact
that even the ravages of consumption are suspended during pregnancy.   Diseases during this
period may be common enough, but so far from
being *natural to that condition*, they are merely
the evidences of *unnatural* habit or circumstances
of the individual.   Under ordinary healthful conditions, and with proper observance of hygienic
management in all its details, the different stages
of pregnancy should progress with an even tenor
and terminate without any serious sickness.

MIDWIVES — MALE AND FEMALE.

History informs us that in Greece, Rome,
Persia, Egypt, Arabia, and Chaldea, woman was
woman's physician.   The Old Testament tells us
that female midwifery was an honorable calling
among the ancient Hebrews.   Since the begin-

13

ning of history, says Mrs. C. M. Dall, the lives of
eighty-seven women, eminent not only for obstetrical skill, but capable of extended general
practice, have been written.

According to universal experience in this matter, the success of female *accoucheurs* has been at
least as great as that of male practitioners, and
statistics of all ages show that the attendance of
women has been accompanied with fewer accidents and a less number of fatal cases than the
practice of man.

Except in most parts of Great Britain and the
United States, the general practice of midwifery
is still in the hands of women. In some
European countries the business is divided, but
in the greater number of countries on earth,
civilized and uncivilized, woman officiates in all
ordinary cases. In Russia, educated females
attend all classes of society, from the Imperial
family down to the most humble serf or ex-serf.
The Chinese employ midwives as a rule, obstetrical surgeons being called upon only when
instrumental assistance is positively necessary.
The American Indian, the Otaheiteans, the New
Zealanders, and many other nations and tribes
who employ female midwives or nobody, are
celebrated for easy births and exemption from
accidents. Omitting the long line of obstetrical

talent amongst the ancients, and noted female
practitioners and authors of obstetrical work
from the beginning of the Christian era in
the old countries up to the eighteenth century, we find that old Mrs. Wiat, who died
at Dorchester, Massachusetts, in 1705, aged
ninety-four years, attended as midwife in more
than eleven hundred cases. Mrs. Whittemore,
who died in Marlboro, Vermont, at the age of
eighty-seven, often traveled through the woods on
snowshoes to attend her patients, and of more
than two thousand births she never lost a case.
Mrs. Elizabeth Phillips, who was born at West-
minster, England, and commissioned to act as
midwife by the Lord Bishop of London in 1718,
removed to Charleston, Massachusetts, the following year, where her gravestone now records the
honorable story that she assisted in successfully
bringing into the world more than three thousand
children. Mrs. Jane Alexander, who died at Boston in 1845, aged sixty-one years, studied obstetrics with Dr. James Hamilton, of Edinburgh
and practiced in this country twenty-five years
without losing a patient. Mrs. Stebbins, who
died at Westfield, Massachusetts, in 1844, at the
age of seventy-five, was an extensive and successful practitioner for many years. Many similar
facts could be added to bring this record up to

the present time, but we beg to let the foregoing
at present suffice.

While we advocate the restoration of the practice of midwifery to well-trained females, we are
far from desiring to see it taken from the hands
of educated physicians and entrusted to ignorant
nurses. We hold, however, that all females
should be sufficiently intelligent on this subject
to manage an ordinary labor, and certainly the
education required for this purpose is exceedingly
simple. It is very true, though, that a multitude
of disorders and deformities existing in artificial
society of our times do render surgical assistance
often necessary; and for this purpose the practical surgeon *accoucheur* should be retained for
complications and emergencies. The reason that
not many young women are properly educated
or perfectly trained, is because the immense influence of an interested profession is arrayed
against them.

During pregnancy, there is an increased excitement and exertion in all the vital functions of the
system. At the earlier stages, we observe a state
of illness, and at the latter stage a stronger,
healthier action of nature. It would seem as if,
at the commencement of pregnancy, nature makes
a collection in all parts of the system, and that
she levies a contribution on them. Even the

nerves seem willing to assist the new process of life; those of the stomach, and the senses particularly, are much affected and irritated. What else can this sickness in the stomach and the increasing appetite mean? What of this desire for certain food, which will not cease till satisfied? What does it mean when eyes, ears, nose, and palate have their distinct desires and distinct aversions? Why is a new, unknown feeling awakened in a mother that makes her carefully watch over a still uncertain future? Why does her sleep become uneasy, and why is she now more wakeful during nights than before, and hear in her sleep the slightest noise, which formerly could not disturb her?

We have partly lifted the veil that nature has thrown over her most mysterious work. The augmented action of the system produces a greater appetite, a higher degree of bodily heat, and increased excretion and secretion of waste substance. It is indicated by nature that cleanliness of the skin must be an important object in the dietetical regimen of a pregnant mother. As the heat of the body in these conditions seems to be more marked, it is contrary to nature to use warm water for that purpose, because the heat of the body and water for that purpose, as like brought to like, effects a mere assimilation.

Without strife between different temperatures of different bodies there can be no reaction. The skin would become flabby, and a flabby skin during pregnancy would endanger the health of the fœtus, produce disease, or even cause its death. It is, therefore, necessary that the daily ablutions should be performed or begun with water not higher than 75° and lowered gradually to 70° or 65° Fahrenheit, in order to increase and strengthen the action as well as the circulation of the capillaries of the skin. Spine, abdomen, breasts, particularly the nipples, should be washed with regularity, the latter several times a day with cold water, and the whole surface of the body gently rubbed after the bath by another healthy person. Formerly, when hydro-therapeutics were not fully understood and appreciated, the washing of these parts with alcoholic liquids was recommended. This practice is now considered unsafe. The alcohol penetrates the body by absorption, and being a violent narcotic, it will effect the ganglionic nerves as readily as if it had been taken by the mouth.

The proper beverage for a pregnant mother is water; fresh, pure water, or milk, if from a healthy cow. Coffee, tea, and other hot drinks are decidedly injurious if taken habitually. During nursing they must be positively forbidden, because they provoke a profusion of unhealthy milk, impairing the health of the child, whose absorbing system is irritated thereby. Many physicians of recognized authority are of the opinion that scrofulous diseases, which have spread so much among the human race, can be traced to the time when tea and coffee came into use, and their effects were communicated to the infant. Teas of all kinds should be kept out of the sick-room, and especially green tea. The Chemical Society of London has at different times analyzed green tea, and it has been demonstrated and proven by chemical evidence that the glazing or coloring matter consists principally of Prussian blue and gypsum. So that, in fact, the drinkers of green tea, as it comes to our markets, indulge in a beverage of Chinese paint, and one might easily imitate this mixture by dissolving Prussian blue and plaster of paris in hot water. The Chinese themselves do not drink this tea,— they only sell it.

Frequently, by the increased action of the system, induced by daily bathing and drinking of fresh water, with proper exercise in the open air, the skin will throw out old waste matter in the form of eruptions or boils, especially when daily ablutions were not regularly observed at other times. This will be of the greatest benefit to the child, as it will purify and free tne circulation of the mother from all hereditary predisposition to disease. We will not repeat here our views on diet; the food should be plain but nutritious, and well selected according to individual observations. Condiments and so-called appetizers must be discarded. Spices, like pepper, ginger, cinnamon, cloves, cayenne, mustard, if used at all, should be used very sparingly; nutmeg is poison to the female system, and must be avoided. Vinegar, as prepared by many distilleries in this country, is made deleterious by having an addition of vitriol and cayenne in order to make it more acrid. All persons guilty of adulterating articles used in food have not been hung yet, or prosecuted as criminals, as they should be.

The most important duty of a pregnant mother consists in proper and daily exercise in the open air. Nothing prospers from indolence or under the influence of impure air, which fills most sitting-rooms and heated houses. Most young women in the higher ranks of society avoid all active exercise; and more than ever if their condition becomes a burden to them. Brought up in an unnatural effeminacy, their muscular system has neither been developed nor accustomed to exertion. In their state of pregnancy, therefore, they feel so uncomfortable as to be unable to endure an active life. If they expose themselves to the air at all, they do so by sitting still in an easy carriage. Others, belonging to the class of busy housekeepers, have no time for sitting still, much less for going out in the open air. Both parties act contrary to nature, and injure both themselves and the child that reposes under their hearts. Riding in a comfortable open carriage on good roads has its enjoyment as a passive exercise, but it omits all proper use of the limbs and muscles, while their wholesome activity is absolutely necessary, in order to prevent the whole organic structure from sinking into debility. All natural powers decrease and cease through want of exercise, and especially organic power. The magnet, kept in a box, instead of being in constant use, loses its power of attraction; this power, on the other hand, will increase as the weight attached to it is, from time to time, made heavier. While all the lighter exercises of the gymnasium are strongly recommended for girls and women of all ages, of course modified by a trained instructor according to age and constitutional vigor, in pregnancy, walking, properly systematized, stands supreme, because in its effects it has a direct bearing upon those organs most actively participating in the final act.

The proper time for enjoying these exercises is
to be regulated according to the season of the
year. During the fall and winter months, from
ten to twelve in the morning should be selected,
while during the warmer days the evening hours
may be adopted. If dinner is the principal meal,
a bodily and mental repose thereafter is to be
observed. We draw attention to the chapter on
Air in this connection. Another class of young
mothers, quite unaware of what may hurt them,
because they are extremely thoughtless and
believe that their general good health will permit
them to engage in excessive activity, have often
been sorely punished. They will lift weights,
handle baskets full of clothes, or buckets full of
water, reaching for articles which require raising
their hands high above their body, etc. They
are even reckless enough to mount a horse or put
on a corset and go to a dance. The author
himself, disgusting as it may appear, was, on one
occasion, the witness of a miscarriage and premature delivery in a ballroom, several years ago.
No words are strong enough to censure such
conduct. Every prospective young mother ought
to ponder the unfortunate consequences of a
miscarriage; it is often the cause of those horrible
uterine diseases. An abortion once brought on
by such gross imprudence, will repeat itself by

action less objectionable, and the person guilty of it might never become a mother *de facto.*

Of riding in a carriage as a mere passive exercise, we have spoken above, as having but little to recommend it in general; it is most objectionable, however, in the second part and towards the end of pregnancy. Still less proper in this delicate situation is riding on horseback, even when done by walking the horse. It may be that the horse does not make a false step, but the whole sexual system becomes excited by this kind of exercise when it should be kept uniformly quiet.

All the rules in the last part of this chapter should also be observed during the time of nursing. A mother ought not to offer the breast to her infant under any state of excitement or when she is fatigued. Finally, let her keep in mind that it is always offensive to refined society to see a pregnant or nursing mother engage in violent pastimes.

We must not, in this connection, omit referring to the "sitz-bath," its application and great value in pregnancy. For invigorating the pelvic organs, for perfect local cleanliness, and for inducing proper exercise, nothing can serve to greater advantage. They should be taken every other day in addition to a general ablution. Temperature, beginning with 75°, gradually lowering to 65°,

Fahrenheit. Duration, from twenty to thirty minutes.

To make the happiness of a young mother complete in all its fullness, it becomes necessary that it should be her privilege, good fortune, and ability to furnish the first sustenance to the newborn from her own breast. When, however, on account of circumstances, natural or otherwise, which it is impossible to overcome, this glory should be denied her, the milk of a healthy and *fresh* cow, properly diluted, has to be substituted. If its supply cannot be made reliable in its uniform delivery, the best grade of condensed milk is preferable. It is essential that it should be prepared and given at a proper and always the same temperature—96–98° Fahrenheit.

CHOICE OF SEX.

If the simple announcement of our subject in this chapter does not predispose the reader to a favorable hearing, we do not intend to secure it by urging any extraneous reasons for its legitimate place in this book. The race of prudish people is not yet extinct, and there may be a few among the many thousands whose squeamishness may condemn the popular treatment of one of the most vital questions concerning the future happiness of the human family. However, we feel

confident that a sufficient number of our readers
will remain to satisfy our highest ambition, who
will appreciate our motive in presenting this
topic in chaste and fitting terms, and without
violating the refinement or true modesty of any
good Christian man or woman.

A lady of Boston had become intensely interested in Napoleon and his exploits, reading
everything relating to him, and bore a son during
his triumphal career. He inherited the most
decided martial tastes, and became so enthusiastic
in his admiration of "Nap," that he covered
the walls of his rooms with pictures of him and
his battles.

The case of Napoleon himself furnishes a
similar illustration: his mother, while pregnant,
having shared with her husband the dangers of a
military campaign.

A lady in New York, possessing a good brain
and an active temperament, was employed pro-
fessionally as a teacher of music. Her husband
had a fine temperament and a well-balanced brain,
too, but his talents for music was rather moderate. They had several children born to them
while the mother was in the full practice of her
profession, and all of them had superior musical
abilities, mastering several instruments almost by
instinct. We could carry these examples over an

indefinite number of pages, but feel disinclined to tire the reader by the sameness of their penetration.

It is a popularly known historical fact that the sages of ancient Greece understood the doctrine of fetal impressions; and that they saw clearly that the work of perfecting the physical man should begin before his birth, is evident from their teachings. They directed that women should devoutly worship Apollo, Narcissus, Castor, Pollux, and others, all deified personifications of masculine beauty. And the fair and pious daughters of Attica placed the statues of these gods in their bedchambers, and fixing their eyes upon their forms and their features of ideal purity, adored them with loving fervor. Yet neither the ancients nor the disciples of modern sciences have ever approached satisfactorily the great problem now before us.

Why is it that Great Britain has nine hundred thousand more women and girls than she has boys and men? or that, in the German Empire, they count over one million females in excess of males? or why the weaker sex in Norway and Sweden has a majority of nearly three hundred thousand on their side? In old communities, the latest census presents the same disproportion everywhere. In the United States, according to the *total* census, we have nearly a million more males than females; yet, Massachusetts has eighty thousand maidens, fair and lovely, in excess of local demand. Nearly the same ratio can be accepted for the older States in general. All these stubborn facts of numerical mismanagement will be elucidated and made to appear plausible in the course of the following lines.

For more than a thousand years physiological investigations have been actively applied to discover the exact laws by which the procreative powers are governed in producing the sex in the fœtus. The author joined this army of anxious inquisitors, about thirty years ago, and he has since experimented at various times on animals of different kinds with methodical exactness, until he has now become fairly and positively convinced that physiology, and the laws thereof, have very little to do with it, but that nature's great secret is performed by a purely "psychological combustion."

A thorough knowledge of the doctrines laid down and recommended in several previous chapters, together with the practical hints and directions given on the pages of this one, will put it within the power of parents to predetermine, to an almost unlimited and certain extent, not only the mental and moral qualities of their descendants, but also, and through these, their physical condition and their sex.

It is a lamentable, yet indisputable, fact that in the propagation of the human species conception, ninety-five times in a hundred, takes place during the mere exercise of and free indulgence in animal propensities or sexual passions—accidentally, and herein lies all the mischief of numerical disproportion of the sexes. The spirit involved at the time, the intense desire to satisfy perhaps the most legitimate and purest ambition, generally leaves out all thought and calculation as to its natural sequence or its logical effect. The sex of the fœtus is determined by the one who, during the process, displays the most vitalizing force and affection, and whose influence is the strongest during and in the consummation of the act; and that side will always and positively produce the opposite sex. Thus, if the tendency referred to is represented in the male, the germ developed will be that of the female sex, and *vice versa. Vice versa?* "There's the rub." Because these conditions, inclinations, and propensities are much oftener present on the male side than the opposite, it follows that by continual free and thoughtless indulgence, the preponderance of female births must be accepted as a natural conclusion. Such is the author's opinion and firm conviction after many years of close observation and of numerous and varied experiments.

If amativeness is strongly represented on the female side, while at the same time some degree of constitutional indifference can be traced on the opposite, the male children will invariably be in the ascendency; while in a union where these threads of nature and character are evenly balanced, the sexes will alternate.

The most unfortunate feature of human passion, in connection with gross ignorance,—we may justly call it human depravity,—is the fact that husbands addicted to the use of stimulants will frequently court genital intercourse when in a state of intoxication. We are not inclined to dwell in detail upon the consequences of such misdeeds; they are obvious, and point to the greatest curse of intemperance. Its baneful influence in this direction fills our asylums, it degenerates the nation, and taxes the commonwealth most unjustly.

The time and conditions for these grave responsibilities should be well chosen; let the mind and heart be cheerful, body in its best state, surroundings pleasant and serene, and love, pure and blissful, on either side, the only inspiration.

The practical value of lofty truths as here enunciated, we hope, will be fully appreciated. Children may be brought into this world intelli-

14

gent or stupid, amiable or ill-tempered, beautiful or homely, male or female, at will. It is equally true that any particular quality of organization, contour, figure, or cast of features, even though feebly or not at all developed in the parents, may, through the instrumentality of the means indicated in the first part of this chapter, be imparted to their offspring. In making these statements, however, we should not be understood as underrating health and corporeal beauty as valuable and important parental qualifications.

Lastly, we have no right to usher either physically or mentally deformed children into life of bodily pain or mental suffering. The means of perfecting our offspring are in our hands, and we are responsible for their use. No child should be the offspring of weakness or apathy, of indifference, or of *accidental combinations*, much less of organic disorder, perverted passions, or brutal instinct; but of health, activity, sincerity, purity, sweetness, harmony, and beauty.

APPENDIX.

As ANNOUNCED in the chapter on Food, we herewith place before our readers the famous "Beaumont Tables" on time of digestion, adding to it the table of nutriment as contained in the various articles of everyday diet from the Physiology of Professor Tiedemann.

From the investigation made by Dr. Beaumont, it appears that the following articles were converted into chyle (digested), namely:

	Hours.	Min.
Rice (boiled soft), tripe, pig's feet...............................	1	00
Apples (sweet and ripe)...	1	30
Venison..	1	35
Sago (boiled)..	1	45
Tapioca, barley, bread, cabbage, milk (boiled), bread and milk (cold)..	2	00
Potatoes (roasted), parsnips (boiled)...........................	2	10
Oysters (undressed), eggs (raw)................................	2	13
Turkey, goose..	2	30
Apple dumplings...	3	00
Eggs (boiled soft), beef, mutton (roasted)....................	3	00
Bread—Corn (baked), carrots (boiled).........................	3	15
Potatoes, turnips (boiled), butter and cheese.................	3	30
Pork (boiled), oysters (stewed)................................	3	30
Eggs (boiled hard, or fried), fowls (domestic)................	4	00
Fowls (wild), pork (salted and boiled).........................	4	30
Veal (roasted), pork, beef (salted and roasted)...............	5	30

It may be stated here, that in an unhealthy or debilitated stomach these articles would probably be much longer undergoing digestion. It should

211

also be borne in mind that the most nutritious articles may not always assimilate the most easily or afford most strength. Certain combinations of diet will operate often more favorably in one case than in another.

The comparative nutriment contained in the various kinds of food is a subject of great importance, and its knowledge and observation should be considered indispensable to the art of cookery. The following tabular view is the proportion in every 1,000 parts:

Mutton	298	Beet root	148
Beef	260	Carrots	98
Haddock	180	Turnips	42
Milk	72	Cucumbers	25
Nuts	930	Chicken	270
Barley	920	Veal	350
Beans (dry)	890	White of egg	130
Bread	800	Wheat	950
Oats	742	Peas (dry)	930
Pork	240	Molasses	866
Grapes	270	Rice	880
Potatoes	120	Almonds	656
Peaches	200	Rye	792
Apples	170	Plums	290
Codfish	210	Strawberries	120
Apricots	260	Cabbage	73
Cherries	250	Melons	30
Gooseberries	190	Beans (green)	170
Peas (green)	160	Blood	215

This table of nutriment, as actually contained in the various articles of food, is from the pen of one of the foremost men of Heidelberg University, but by no means furnished with the intention of making people believe that the greatest amount of nutriment in one or the other article is a reason for its preference as food. Much depends upon the process of preparation and proper compounding in order to make digestion easy and assimilation possible. According to Prout, who first brought this whole matter to clear terms, milk, which contains only seventy-three parts of nutrition, is the only substance thoroughly prepared by nature as a *ready nutriment*.

CARD.

As STATED in the closing of the first chapter of the work, we shall always be pleased to design and describe individual exercises for children or adults, as hygienic measures, or for the relief of chronic disorders, for deformities, or for especial development of separate parts of the body. We have so far abstained from furnishing any general directions or specified prescriptions, because we do emphatically believe in the doctrine of Alexander Von Humboldt. The human family cannot properly be classified. In health or in sickness, we are a society of individuals, not of classes. Much mischief is done and great sums of money are wasted by the people who read the alluring advertisements of quacks and empirics, and without much thinking or reflection, they are ever ready to experiment, generally believing in the trite saying that "what is good for the goose must be good for the gander"—and for his cousins or his aunts, too. The most rational, the most dangerous, or the most harmless remedies will not act alike in any two different cases. Take rheumatism, for instance. While it cannot be radically cured by any drug system, we have various means by which acute attacks can be shortened or considerably relieved, yet every well-informed physician knows that while a certain prescription in one person may act promptly and favorably, in another it remains utterly without effect, or that the same remedy, in the same case, at another time, will be found inoperative under conditions and symptoms precisely the same.[1]

It is then admitted and stands to reason that every case of sickness or physical disorder should be treated on its own merits, according to its individual history and conditions, and more especially so when the treatment is by movements or therapeutic gymnastics. Age, weight, general vigor, sex, personal habits, and many other points, are to be intelligently considered, and must govern the character of these exercises in quality and quantity.

We will, at the same time, be accessible to families or individuals who are not complete strangers to hydro-therapeutics, regarding the *modus operandi* of various applications, tendering to them our views and advice in all chronic diseases, when a combination of the two (medical movements and therapeutic baths) is favorably indicated, and prescribe accordingly. Yet, while

[1] Sufferers with this malady have only one avenue open to them for a perfect cure: Hydro-therapeutics in connection with Russian or Turkish baths, under a strict and very abstemious discipline, with plenty of time and patience at their disposal.

we hold that the scientific, or medical, part of Ling's system should be permanently incorporated in, or identified with, rational hydro-therapeutics, we wish it to be understood that some cases may not always require both.

We have often, by request, arranged a small home gymnasium, where a good-sized room, with high ceiling, has been available, either for the use of the family, or at times with apparatus for specific purposes. The same demand has frequently engaged our supervision in supplying means for outdoor gymnasia, in the yard, or on the lawn. These facilities can generally be put up in any home without much outlay. The money invested will soon return in the reduction of doctor fees and apothecary bills, but the benefit derived therefrom by the young ones is for a lifetime.

What is said in the chapter on Hygiene in Matrimony, or in the one on Sex and Disproportion thereof, may frequently require supplementary directions, applying to individual cases, which will be cheerfully furnished on application.

All letters of such inquiries should be directed to the author personally,—Dr. William A. Jansen, Miamisburg, Ohio, and must contain postage to secure reply.

For copies of the book,—$1.50 postpaid,— address H. R. Publishing Company, Box No. 25, Miamisburg, Ohio.